Nathaniel Fludd

Nathaniel Fludd
BEASTOLOGIST

BOOK FOUR

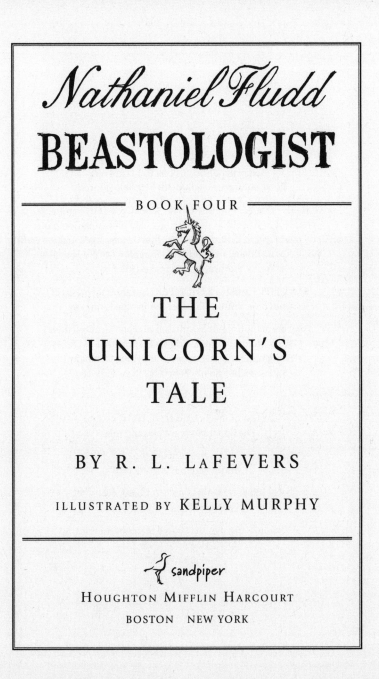

THE
UNICORN'S
TALE

BY R. L. LaFEVERS

ILLUSTRATED BY KELLY MURPHY

sandpiper

HOUGHTON MIFFLIN HARCOURT
BOSTON NEW YORK

SANDPIPER and the SANDPIPER logo are trademarks of
Houghton Mifflin Harcourt Publishing Company.

For information about permission to reproduce selections
from this book, write to Permissions,
Houghton Mifflin Harcourt Publishing Company,
215 Park Avenue South, New York, New York 10003.

www.hmhbooks.com

The text of this book is set in ITC Giovanni.
The illustrations are pen and ink.

The Library of Congress Cataloging-in-Publication
Control Number 2010025118

ISBN: 978-0-547-48277-4 hardcover
ISBN: 978-0-547-85079-5 paperback

Manufactured in the United States of America
DOC 10 9 8 7 6 5 4 3 2
4500424427

THIS BOOK IS DEDICATED TO MY GRANDMOTHER,

PRINCESS GARBUTT,

WHO TUCKED ME SAFELY UNDER HER WING AND

WHISKED ME OFF

ON MANY WONDERFUL ADVENTURES,

PROVIDING A SAFE HAVEN

WHENEVER LIFE GOT OVERWHELMING.

—R.L.L.

FOR MY ANIMAL-LOVING NIECE, ANNA.

—K.M.

Chapter One

OCTOBER 1928

"*I STILL DON'T UNDERSTAND* why we had to come to France," Nate grumbled as he dragged his rucksack on the ground behind him. Not liking the bumpy ride, his pet gremlin, Greasle, scampered up the pack's buckles and straps to Nate's shoulder.

"We came to France because our lives can't stand still while we wait for news of Obediah Fludd to surface," Aunt Phil explained. "We still have a job to do, Nate. And today, being a beastologist brings us to France."

She stopped walking and Nate bumped into her. "Sorry," he mumbled, embarrassed.

Aunt Phil reached out a hand to steady him. "We have scouts everywhere, keeping an eye out for Obediah. If he's spotted, we'll know soon enough. Now, pull yourself together. We've work to do."

Cornelius, Aunt Phil's talking dodo, sniffed. "If the boy were a true Fludd, he wouldn't snivel so much."

As Nate glared at him, Greasle piped up. "Seems to me there was a certain dodo doing an awful lot of sniveling this morning. Something about nots wanting to be left home alone."

Cornelius raised his beak into the air and fluffed his feathers. "I wasn't sniveling. I was being cautious. I'd already been attacked once, you know."

"You weren't attacked!" Greasle scoffed. "A door accidentally falled on you."

"Enough!" Aunt Phil said.

"He started it," the gremlin muttered.

Nate let himself fall a few paces behind and lowered his voice. "Bickering with Cornelius is not going to help convince Aunt Phil to let me keep you," he pointed out.

Greasle's shoulders drooped. "I know. But I can't stand it when that overstuffed pigeon be's mean to you."

"Are you two planning on joining us anytime soon?" Cornelius drawled.

Nate looked up to see that the dodo and Aunt Phil had reached the farmhouse, and he hurried to catch up. A flock of chickens had stopped scratching in the dirt to stare curiously at Cornelius.

Nate sent the dodo a sly look. "Relatives of yours, Cornelius?"

The dodo clacked his beak in annoyance.

"Don't worry about him," Greasle told the chickens. "He's just a big fat chicken who can't even lay eggs."

Just as Aunt Phil whirled around to give everyone another scolding, the farmhouse door burst open. A short, round man tumbled out into the yard. He wore a black cap and smelled of garlic and sausage. "Dr. Fludd! I had nearly despaired of your arrival!"

"I'm sorry, Monsieur Poupon. We came as soon as we got your message. It does take an hour or two to cross the channel—even in an airplane. Now, what's all this about a guivre infestation?"

"Le dragon showed up in my well two days ago and won't budge."

"One guivre can hardly be considered an infestation," Aunt Phil pointed out. "Besides, you *are* having an unseasonably warm autumn. Perhaps this one just needs to cool off for a bit—"

"*Non!* He may not cool off in my well. Le guivre, he carries disease, the plague! All my family, my animals, will become sick if you do not remove him at once."

"Nonsense." Aunt Phil bristled. "That is merely an old rumor started in the Middle Ages. It has long been proven false. Guivres carry no diseases."

The farmer's face grew red and he clenched his fists. "Are you saying you won't remove him?"

"No. I am simply pointing out that you have nothing to fear but inconvenience. Come along, Nate. Let's go see to the guivre. We'll let you know when we've finished, Monsieur Poupon."

With that, Aunt Phil headed back down the walkway. "I don't want that poor guivre around him any longer than necessary," she muttered to herself.

She was so annoyed with the farmer that she marched right past the path leading to the well. Not wanting this to take any longer than it had to, Nate stopped and called her back. "I think this is the way," he said, pointing to a low wall of thick gray stone.

"Now, that *is* clever," Cornelius drawled. "Finding a well in plain sight. I take back everything I ever said about your lack of Fludd skills."

"If you can't say something helpful, then don't say

anything at all," Aunt Phil told the dodo. To Nate, she said, "Thank you."

When they came to a stop in front of the well, Greasle whispered in Nate's ear, "What's a guivre, anyway?"

"I don't know," he said. "But we're about to find out. Now, be quiet so I can pay attention." He didn't want to miss a thing. Aunt Phil might quiz him on it later. Or it could turn out to be a matter of life and death. One never knew with her.

She set her pack on the ground, then leaned over the well. "Hello?" she called out, her voice echoing down into the dark depths.

In answer, a great gushing stream of water shot out of the well. Aunt Phil leaped back, avoiding the hosing. Unfortunately, Nate didn't. The jet of water cascaded down on his head.

"Sorry about that," Aunt Phil said as he wiped the water from his eyes. "I should have warned you."

Nate wrung the water from his coat, glad they were having a warm autumn. On his shoulder, Greasle gave a quick shake, flinging the water from her oily skin.

Aunt Phil turned back to the well. "Thank you, dear, but I didn't need any water today," she called down. "I actually wanted to have a little chat with you. Do you have a moment?"

The splashing stopped, then slowly, something big and slithery began to rise up out of the well's depths.

Chapter Two

A POINTED GRAY SNOUT EMERGED. It was followed by a smooth, round head with fleshy horns on either side where ears should have been. His eyes were large and round and had very long eyelashes. They made him look rather cute, Nate thought. If you didn't count the fact that he was snakelike and thicker than Nate's whole body. "Is he scared of us?" Nate asked Aunt Phil.

"No, just shy. He's worried we'll try to frighten him by removing our clothes."

Nate gaped at her. "Why would we do that?"

"People used to think that taking off their clothes and waving their arms and generally acting like idiots would scare guivres away. Another old wives' tale, I'm afraid. Now, do you have those fish we brought?"

"In here," Nate said, patting the basket that hung from his side.

"And right ripe they are," Greasle whispered, pinching her nose.

"Very well," Aunt Phil said. "I want you to take one out and jiggle it. Be sure the guivre sees it, and once he has, slowly back away. With luck, he'll be so hungry that he'll follow the fish. Once he's out of the well, I'll catch him in the net and we can safely relocate him."

"O-okay." Wondering if the guivre had any teeth, Nate reached into the basket and pulled out a cold, slimy fish. Wrinkling his nose, he held it as far out in front of him as possible.

"Here you go," he said, giving the fish a vigorous jiggle. The sudden movement startled the guivre so badly, he dived back into the well.

"Gently, Nate. You don't want him to think the fish is attacking."

"Sorry," he mumbled. He jiggled the fish again, this time more daintily. The guivre slowly peeked back over the edge of the stone wall, then tilted his head to study the fish. A tongue snaked out, and the serpentine body began to ooze out of the well, longer and bigger than Nate had even imagined. When the creature had uncoiled, he was twice as long as Aunt Phil, and Nate was filled with an overwhelming urge to run away. Only Cornelius's sneering gaze held him in place. He'd show that dodo who the real chicken was.

"That's it." Aunt Phil's voice was encouraging. "Just a little bit farther now . . . Perfect!"

On the word *perfect*, she cast the net over the guivre. The dragon bucked and wiggled like a live electrical wire, making it impossible for Aunt Phil to get a decent hold. In the end, she had to throw herself on top of the writhing creature. "Give him the fish, Nate! Quick!"

Nate tossed the fish at the guivre. He stopped midstruggle, opened his mouth, and neatly caught the fish, all in one fluid motion. That gave Aunt Phil just enough time to get the net secure. "Good job," she huffed, then pushed to her feet. "We'll each take an end and carry him back to the plane. We flew over a nice lake a short ways back. We'll relocate him there."

Nate tried to grab hold of his end, but the guivre slapped his tail back and forth playfully, like a kitten. "Hold still," Nate grunted. Finally, in desperation, he flung himself on the tail, trapping it beneath his body.

He and Aunt Phil trudged back to the plane, the guivre bucking and twisting the whole time. Cornelius followed, calling out unhelpful directions. "Watch out for that rock. There. Yes, *that* one. Pick up your feet!"

By the time they reached Aunt Phil's Sopwith, Nate felt as if he'd been in a wrestling match.

"On three," Aunt Phil said. "One, two, *three!*" On the

final count, Aunt Phil gave a mighty heave. Nate had no choice but to do the same. With a dull thump, the guivre landed on the floor of the cargo hold. Aunt Phil quickly shut the hatch. "There," she said, wiping her hands on her pants. "That wasn't too hard, was it?"

Nate agreed. Compared to some of the things they'd done—such as chase down the basilisk—that had been downright easy.

"You stay here," Aunt Phil said. "I'm going to tell Monsieur Poupon we've finished up."

Nate knelt and tried to wipe his hands off on the grass.

"Hey, look," Greasle said, pointing at the horizon. "A bird what can *fly!*"

Cornelius pointedly ignored her, but Nate looked up. Something was headed their way, but it wasn't flying like any sort of bird he'd ever seen. It zigged and zagged crazily, slowly losing altitude, as if it could barely stay in the air. It pointed its little beak at the plane, gave one final flap of its wings, and belly-flopped onto the hood with an audible *oomph*. It lifted its head long enough to give one feeble coo, then lay gasping for air.

Greasle scampered forward. "It's not food!" Nate called out, remembering the last carrier pigeon Greasle had met.

"I knows," the gremlin said scornfully over her shoulder. "It's one of them carrier pigeons." She lifted one of its wings, then let go. It flopped lifelessly on the plane.

As Nate drew closer, he saw a small scroll tied to the bird's left foot. The pigeon cooed again. "I think it wants us to read the message."

Another coo of agreement.

Nate's heart began to beat faster. Maybe it was news of Obediah. Maybe he'd finally been spotted and they'd have a chance to ask him some questions!

Hands trembling with excitement, Nate reached down and gently untied the note. The poor little pigeon gave one last faint coo, then fell silent.

Shoving the note into his pocket, Nate grabbed the canteen from his rucksack and poured some water into the lid. He lifted the pigeon's head and dribbled a few drops of water down the exhausted bird's throat. It cooed again, this time a little bit stronger.

The pigeon seen to, Nate retrieved the note from his pocket and unrolled it.

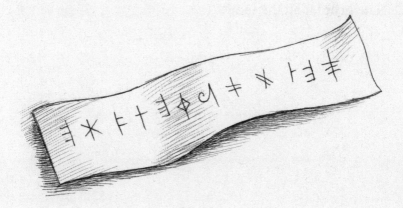

"What's that?" Greasle asked, staring down at the strange marks on the paper.

"I don't know. Code, maybe?"

"It looks like one of them chickens walked through a mud puddle, then did a little dance," Greasle said.

Nate felt a small jab on his arm. When he looked up, Cornelius was craning his neck, trying to see the note. "I bet I know what it is. Let me have a look."

Nate tilted the note in the dodo's direction. Cornelius studied it with one bright yellow eye, then sniffed. "Ogham," he announced. "It's ogham script. A very old form of writing used by those who live in the forests. Philomena will know how to read it."

Even if you don't. The dodo didn't actually say that, but Nate heard it all the same.

Chapter Three

IGNORING THE DODO'S UNSPOKEN SNUB, Nate ran up the path to the house. Aunt Phil met him halfway. "Ho-ho! Where are you going in such a hurry?"

"A note," Nate huffed. "A pigeon came with a note. Maybe there's news of Obediah?" There was nothing he wanted more than to track down the one man who might know something about what had happened to his parents. Nate handed Aunt Phil the message, then nearly danced with impatience while he waited for her to read it.

When she was done, she gave a small shake of her head. "It's not about Obediah, I'm afraid."

"It's not?" Nate's excitement whooshed out of him like a deflating balloon.

"No. It's from Mr. Sylvan, the caretaker of Broceliande forest. There is a problem with the unicorn. It seems she's been acting quite oddly and Mr. Sylvan is afraid she might be ill."

Not only was it *not* about Obediah, but it was something that would distract Aunt Phil from pursuing him! And while a unicorn was interesting, it didn't seem nearly as interesting to Nate as finding out more about his parents. "That's too bad she's sick, but people and animals get sick all the time."

"Actually, Nate, unicorns never get sick. They are famous for their healing abilities. For a unicorn to become ill is very serious indeed."

Nate's heart sank. "We're going to go to this forest place, aren't we?"

"We have to, Nate. If one of the last unicorns on earth is unwell, it's up to us to tend to her." Her voice held a note of gentle reproach.

Nate had an idea. "Do you think Obediah made the unicorn get sick?"

Aunt Phil thought for a moment. "I don't think so. The caretaker would have known about any intruder."

"Maybe not," Nate pointed out. "Dewey didn't know there was an intruder when he called you about the wyverns being on the rampage."

"True, but Mr. Sylvan is very different from Dewey, as you'll soon see."

"But what about Obediah?" The question jumped out of Nate. "It seems to me the longer we wait to go after him, the better chance he'll have of disappearing."

"What would you have me do, Nathaniel? There are a dozen different directions the man could have taken. A dozen different beasts he could be hunting, even as we speak. If we run after the man, there is a very good chance we'll be going in the wrong direction, taking us even farther away from him."

Helpless frustration washed over Nate. He reached out and kicked a small rock. It ricocheted off the stone well, narrowly missing Cornelius. Greasle snickered, but Nate hardly even noticed.

"Now," Aunt Phil continued, "let's get back into the plane and head out. We'll drop the guivre off on the way. There's a lovely river that he'd like, just on the border of Broceliande. We'll take him there instead of the lake."

It was a short flight from the outskirts of Paris to where they were going. In no time, a shadowed forest appeared below, surrounded by a grassy meadow. Aunt Phil pointed the nose of the plane downward and began the descent.

As they drew closer and closer to the ground, Aunt Phil continued to head for the trees. Just as Nate began wondering if she was going to try to fly through them, they hit the meadow with a thud. They finally bounced to a stop, just inches from the forest. "We don't want to have to carry the guivre any farther than we have to," Aunt Phil called back to Nate.

Nate crawled out of the cockpit and grabbed his rucksack. Cornelius blinked his big yellow eyes at him. Nate pretended he didn't know what the dodo wanted. *Let Aunt Phil take care of him, if she was so keen on bringing him along,* Nate thought.

He jumped down to the soft grass below, pausing long enough for Greasle to leap from the plane's wing to his shoulder.

"Nate, would you see to Cornelius while I open the cargo hold?" Aunt Phil called over to him.

Nate huffed out a breath of annoyance, then slowly walked back to the plane. He hated this part.

He climbed back into the cockpit and set his rucksack on the seat. Cornelius climbed up on top of it, like a step stool. "I'll need a little boost, I think."

Nate placed his hands on the dodo's solid backside and pushed. The dodo gave a fluttering hop but didn't quite make it over the side.

"A bigger boost, if you please, and mind the tail feathers!" the dodo said over his shoulder.

He was a surprisingly *dense* bird, and far heavier than he looked. Nate pushed again, this time harder. Maybe too hard. The dodo, propelled by Nate's push and his own

flapping momentum, shot over the side of the plane and landed with a graceless splat. He squawked, then gathered himself clumsily to his feet.

"You're welcome," Nate muttered under his breath, then went to help Aunt Phil with the guivre. He'd rather handle a slippery, floppy dragon than that stupid dodo—at least the guivre didn't think Nate was worthless.

"All right," Aunt Phil said when she spotted Nate. "I'll take the head, you take the tail. The closer we get to the river, the more excited the guivre will get, so you'll need to hang on tightly."

She stepped into the cargo hold and carefully pulled the net-wrapped dragon toward her. Leaving him wrapped in the netting, she grabbed his head, and Nate—after a few tries—managed to snag his tail. "Let's go, then," Aunt Phil said, and headed for the river.

The guivre seemed to have lost some of his energy from being out of water and didn't wriggle quite as much as he had before. Even so, Nate was hot and sweaty by the time they reached the riverbank. When the guivre caught sight of the river, he quickly became overjoyed. He bucked and rolled, trying to get to the water. "Hold on!" Nate laughed. "We're almost there."

"On three," Aunt Phil ordered. "One, two, THREE!" With a gentle swing, they launched the creature out past the riverbank and into the river. Before they had even let go, he was diving into the water, rolling and splashing and corkscrewing until he'd completely disappeared.

Nate smiled at the playful beast. He would never have dreamed a dragon could be so unscary.

Without warning, the guivre burst through the surface of the river one last time and launched a stream of clear, cold water straight at Nate and Aunt Phil. It caught Nate on top of the head, and he spluttered in surprise. Aunt Phil laughed. "You're welcome!" she called out as the guivre dived back beneath the surface.

Chapter Four

AUNT PHIL CAME OVER and put her hand on Nate's shoulder. "Now, that was a job well done."

Enjoying the warm, satisfied feeling inside him, Nate had to agree.

"Let's go find Mr. Sylvan, shall we, and see what's wrong with our unicorn."

A tiny voice spoke in Nate's ear. "Ask her now."

He glanced down at his shoulder. "What?"

"Ask her abouts keeping me while she's all happy about that big worm you just rescued."

Nate glanced nervously at Aunt Phil. The gremlin had a point. His aunt *was* in a good mood. He gathered up his courage and fell into step beside her. "You said we would talk about keeping Greasle as a pet once we finished with the wyverns."

"Oh, Nate, there are too many things to think about right now, with the guivre and the unicorn and Obediah. We'll talk about it later."

Later. Always later, Nate thought with a sigh. They walked along in silence for a while before he spoke again. "Where do you think he went?"

"The unicorn is a she, actually."

"No. Obediah. Where do you think he'll go next?"

Aunt Phil gave a grimace of frustration. "I don't know."

"But if you had to guess . . ." Nate knew he should just be quiet, but he couldn't help himself. It was like an itch he had to scratch.

Aunt Phil shrugged helplessly. "I can't understand what the man is up to, so I can't even begin to predict what he'll do next."

Nate thought about that for a moment. "What'll we do if we can't find him again? How will we ever learn more about my parents' disappearance?" Nate flinched. He hadn't meant to ask that last question out loud.

Aunt Phil stopped walking and turned to put her hands on his shoulders. Nate swallowed nervously. "Nate, if I thought for one moment your parents were still alive, I'd charge off to Spitsbergen myself and look for them. But they're not. Your father would never have given up *The Geographica* if there was a breath left in his body."

"But if Obediah has *The Geographica*, why'd he search your house? Or my house, for that matter?"

"I don't know," Aunt Phil said. "I have no idea how the man's mind works or what exactly he's after. But you have to let go of this idea that your parents are still alive. There is absolutely no evidence to support your belief, and it will only bring you heartache."

She was so certain, Nate realized. So absolutely certain. He was desperate to wipe that certainty off her face. *They are alive!* he wanted to shout. But it was clear she wouldn't change her mind, no matter what he said. He bit down on the inside of his cheek, hoping the pain would distract him from the tangle of hot ugly feelings that were threatening to swamp him.

Sensing his distress, Greasle reached out and stroked his arm.

Aunt Phil gave him a brisk pat on the back. "Besides, Nate, that man won't stay hidden for long. Like a bad penny, that one is. He'll turn up soon enough. Shall I tell you of unicorns while we walk?"

Nate didn't want to talk about unicorns, but apparently he didn't have any choice since she wouldn't talk about Obediah. Not trusting his voice, Nate nodded.

"Unicorns are one of the rarest creatures on earth. Their numbers have dwindled drastically in the past two hundred years, especially the *Unicornis europus*."

Nate found he was interested in spite of himself. "You mean there's more than one kind of unicorn?"

"The exact number of species is a matter of some debate among experts. The *Unicornis europus* is the one you've probably seen in stories and on the tapestries in museums, as it is indigenous to Europe.

unicornis europus

It looks very much like a small horse or large deer with cloven hoofs, a long tufted tail, and a horn sprouting from its forehead. But there are other species as well. One of them, the monocerus, is quite hardy. It is best known as the rhinoceros and thrives on the plains of Africa."

"Rhinos aren't unicorns!"

"Actually, they are. Or one type of unicorn, anyway. It was the rhino that Marco Polo described on his journeys to Asia. And even though no one refers to them as unicorns anymore, they are still hunted for their horns."

"Why would anyone want their horns?" Nate asked.

Cornelius snorted. "Oh, honestly. The boy is hopeless. Why would anyone want their horns, indeed."

unicornis monocerus

"Quiet, you," Aunt Phil told the dodo.

"Oh, looks!" Greasle said, pointing to the sky. "A bird what can fly!"

Cornelius sent the gremlin a quelling glance but shut his beak with a snap.

Aunt Phil cleared her throat in warning to the both of them before continuing. "Unicorn horns are extremely rare and worth quite a lot of money. Queen Elizabeth the First had one that was valued at ten thousand pounds. They are able to remove poison from both food and water. Ground up into powder, they act as a very effective healing agent. Some say they even bestow long life."

"Do the unicorns have to be dead for the horn to work?" Nate asked.

"No, but try telling that to all the rabid hunters over the centuries." Aunt Phil's voice was thick with disgust.

"So wouldn't Obediah want the horn for himself, like he wanted the wyverns' treasure?" Nate knew he needed to stop bringing up Obediah, but he couldn't help it. He braced himself for a scolding, but Aunt Phil's next words surprised him.

unicornis elasmotherium

"Normally I would agree with you, Nate, but you see, according to Mr. Sylvan, the unicorn's symptoms have been growing over the last several weeks, getting especially worse the past two. As you and I both know, Obediah couldn't have been anywhere near her, as he was with us in Africa."

Frustrated at her answer, Nate kicked at a pinecone on the forest floor.

"Now, where was I? Oh, yes. Then there is the *Unicornis elasmotherium*. It is related to the monocerus as the elephant is to the woolly mammoth."

"But I thought the woolly mammoth lived back in the Ice Age," Nate exclaimed.

"Very good, Nate! Yes, they did. But there are reports that the *elasmotherium* lived during recorded history as well. The first and last reported sighting was by Sir Mungo Fludd during his travels through the area we now call Mongolia. He claims to have seen one with his own eyes, being hunted by the local people of the steppes.

"Then, of course, there is the Chinese qilin, which we Western beastologists know very little about. Crespi Fludd, one of Mungo's sons, was the first to hear of this creature

chinese qilin

during his extensive travels to China. It's not very much like other unicorns, having the head of a lion and being covered in green scales. The only true similarity is the long, curling horn that protrudes from its head. In fact, some suspect that it is not a unicorn at all, but a horned chimera."

"What's a key-mee-ruh?" Greasle asked.

Aunt Phil frowned at the question. "It is a three-headed beast from Greece, which I will tell you about some other time. There is also the *Unicornis indicus*," she said, return-ing to unicorns. "But it has been so rarely seen that many beast-ologists doubt that it ever truly existed. The one and only sighting was by Mauro Fludd back in 1481, during his travels through India and Asia." Her sigh was full of long-ing. "I would dearly

unicornis indicus

love to see one. According to Mauro, it was distinct among unicorns in that it was brightly colored. While its body was white, its head was dark red and its eyes dark blue. The horn was on the short side—only one and a half feet versus the more common three to four feet. But the colors! The base of the horn was white, the middle section black, and the sharp tip was crimson." She sighed again. "They say you can even recognize the bones of the creature, as they are the color of cinnabar. Watch your step, now. Some of those branches are rather low."

The forest had grown thick around them. The trees were now so tall that Nate couldn't see the tops of some of them, and they grew so close to each other that their branches were tangled together. It was quiet, too—as if the trees and leaves had absorbed all the sounds around them. The forest floor felt springy underfoot.

It was chilly in the shade of the trees, Nate realized, and reached down to button up his jacket. He could hear Greasle's teeth chattering, so he pulled a clean handkerchief from his pocket and handed it to her. She wrapped it around herself like a blanket.

"Why are there so few unicorns left?" Nate asked.

"Now, that is the sad part of the story, I'm afraid. For one, they were heavily hunted for centuries, everyone wanting a unicorn horn of his own. And if you didn't need the horn's healing powers for yourself, you could always sell it for its weight in gold. But other things affected the unicorn population, not just hunting. As more and bigger cities appeared, they ate into the beasts' forest habitat. Unicorns are very solitary creatures and need large, uncluttered territories. But nowadays, everywhere you look, there is a new village or town springing up, like toadstools after a rain. Then came the Great War." Aunt Phil's face grew very grim.

"Miss Lumpton mentioned the Great War in one of her lessons. The war to end all wars, she called it."

"Let us hope so. That long, bloody battle lasted four years. Not only was it devastating for the people involved, it did terrible things to the unicorn population as well. The sheer horror and death and agony of war affected the unicorns like a poison. The mortars and bombs, the toxic gases released, all of those things took a huge toll on the unicorns. We lost most of the remaining ones during that time."

Nate was silent as he digested this tragedy. War sounded too horrible to imagine.

"Ah, look," Aunt Phil said. "Here's Mr. Sylvan's house now."

Nate looked up to find they were in a small clearing. A cozy little cottage sat backed up against the trees. It had wooden sides, bright blue shutters, and a cheerful yellow door. The window boxes were full of orange and purple flowers, and on the roof, a tiny chimney stuck out at a jaunty angle, like a feather in a cap.

As they drew closer, Nate heard strains of a lovely, haunting melody floating on the air. "Is Mr. Sylvan making that music?" he whispered.

Aunt Phil rolled her eyes. "No, that is Mr. Sylvan's gramophone. *Prelude to the Afternoon of a Faun,* by Debussy. Mr. Sylvan claims it was written in honor of his grandfather."

"I prefer 'Clair de lune,' myself," Cornelius muttered.

Just then, the front door opened and Mr. Sylvan himself stepped out. Nate's mouth fell open.

From the waist up, Mr. Sylvan was shaped like a man, although a strangely dressed one. He wore a tweed vest and a red silk necktie, but no shirt. However, from the waist down . . .

"What happened to his legs?" Greasle whispered.

Nate could only shake his head in surprise. From the waist down, Mr. Sylvan was shaped like a goat.

Chapter Five

"NATE, I'D LIKE YOU TO MEET MR. SYLVAN, caretaker of the forest of Broceliande and head faun of Lodge Two Hundred Forty-Seven."

Mr. Sylvan put his hand out to shake. Nate remembered to close his gaping mouth before grasping it. It was a solid hand, with calluses on the palm.

"Mr. Sylvan, this is my nephew, Nathaniel Fludd, the new beastologist-in-training."

"Very pleased to meet you, I'm sure," Mr. Sylvan said. But Nate was too busy staring at the two small horns sprouting from the top of Mr. Sylvan's head to return the greeting.

However, while Nate was staring at the faun, the faun was staring at the dodo. His eyebrows rose up in puzzlement. "Have you brought me a"—he squinted—"a giant duck, then?"

Perched on Nate's shoulder, Greasle slapped her knee and gave a great guffaw of laughter. The faun glanced at her, rubbed his eyes, then opened them again.

Cornelius gave the faun a cold, disdainful stare. "I am a very rare *Raphus cucullatus*," he said, twitching his tail feathers in annoyance.

"Otherwise known as a dodo," Aunt Phil said dryly. "And I'm afraid he's not a present, but my traveling companion."

"A scaredy-cat is more like it," Greasle muttered in Nate's ear.

"Ah, yes, well, do come in," the faun said, looking a bit dazed. "I imagine you'd like a cup of tea after your journey. Although I had hoped you'd be here a little sooner," he added, with a faint note of reproach.

"We were delayed relocating a guivre," Aunt Phil explained.

"I suppose you relocated him into one of my rivers," Mr. Sylvan said with a sigh.

Aunt Phil grinned. "Yes, actually. Just outside the forest. It's plenty big enough, and most of you lot know enough not to be frightened by him."

Mr. Sylvan's cottage was dark inside and smelled faintly of pipe tobacco. Next to the fireplace, an umbrella stand held a half-dozen long-handled toasting forks. A battered copper kettle full of flowers sat on the only table. Mr. Sylvan removed the flowers, filled the kettle with fresh water, then put it on to boil. "Have a seat, have a seat," he clucked at them.

Nate looked around, but all the chairs were piled high with books and newspapers and notepaper.

"Oh, forgive me." Mr. Sylvan hurried over and dumped the piles onto the floor. "I've been very hard at work on my book."

Nate's eyebrows shot up but he didn't say anything. Mr. Sylvan threw Aunt Phil a worried glance. "Is the boy mute?" he asked in a low voice.

"No," Aunt Phil said with a wry smile. "And he's not deaf, either."

Deciding he should say *something*, Nate cleared his throat. "What sort of book are you writing?" he asked.

"A history on the nature of forests, from a faun's perspective, of course. I don't feel anyone but a faun can truly understand the forest. Ah, there's the kettle." He leaped up, his hooves making a hollow clatter on the wood floor. He sprinkled a handful of tea leaves into the kettle, gave it a stir or two, then poured it into three thick mugs. He handed one to Aunt Phil, then Nate. Nate stared down at the bits of twigs and flower petals floating on the surface and wondered what sort of tea it was. He pretended to take a sip, then set the mug down carefully.

Aunt Phil took a hearty sip of hers, then sighed in satisfaction. "Now, Mr. Sylvan, tell us what is wrong with Luminessa."

"Well, it first started a few weeks ago, when her mood became a bit standoffish."

From what Aunt Phil had told him of unicorns, that didn't sound all *that* unusual. Nate hoped they hadn't been called out here for nothing. "Didn't you say unicorns like to be alone?" he asked Aunt Phil.

But it was Mr. Sylvan who answered. "True enough, Mr. Fludd, but do you know why it is that fauns are caretakers of unicorns?"

"No, sir."

"It's because of this." He stood up and pointed to his goat haunches, which made Nate smile.

Mr. Sylvan smiled back. "We are only half-human. Our other half is also a creature of the forest, much like the unicorn. Because of that, we are only half as threatening to a unicorn as a human. They tolerate our presence fairly well."

"But you say she hasn't been tolerating your presence?" Aunt Phil asked.

"No, she's been irritable and snappish, chasing me away when I come up to check on her. She's also become a right little thief, nicking things that don't belong to her. The first thing I noticed missing was my tablecloth, the lovely chintz one you gave me three Christmases ago. She took it off the clothesline. Next were the tea towels. The following week, she reached that long horn of hers through the window and snagged the pillow off my bed!"

Aunt Phil frowned in consternation. "That *is* odd behavior. Especially for Luminessa."

"And that's not all." The faun shifted uneasily in his chair.

"What else, then?" Aunt Phil asked.

The faun stood up again, his face turning red. "She even took a bite out of *me!* Right here, see?" The faun turned around and presented his hindquarters to Aunt Phil.

"Oh dear! She certainly did." Aunt Phil leaned forward and inspected the area. There was a big bald spot next to his tail. "She didn't break the skin, though, just nipped off some of your fur."

Mr. Sylvan sniffed. "It's not fur, it's hair. You of all people should know that."

"Forgive me," Aunt Phil said, hiding a smile. "That was a poor choice of words. Would you like some salve for it?"

Mr. Sylvan sniffed again as he took his seat with great dignity. "No, thank you." He turned the subject away from his hindquarters. "When she's not attacking me, stealing my things, or chasing me off, she's sleeping."

Aunt Phil shook her head gravely. "You are correct, Mr. Sylvan. This is all most unusual. I am glad you called us."

Nate didn't say anything. All in all, it didn't sound like a big deal to him. So the unicorn was hungry and cranky— that happened to everyone once in a while. It certainly didn't seem more important than chasing after Obediah.

"It is too late to start out for the pasture this afternoon," Aunt Phil said. "I'm afraid we'll have to stay here for the night and start first thing in the morning."

"I'd be honored to have you, ma'am." Mr. Sylvan gave a crisp little bow. "I shall go see what dinner my humble cupboards can offer up for us."

Chapter Six

IN SPITE OF NATE'S MISGIVINGS, they spent a pleasant evening in the faun's cottage. They dined on thick slabs of cheese on even thicker slices of homemade bread that they roasted over the fire using the long toasting forks. Nate had never made his own dinner before and found he quite liked it, even if it was a little crispy around the edges and the hot cheese burned the roof of his mouth.

Greasle managed to get melted cheese in her hair, so after dinner, Nate spent half an hour trying to pick it all out.

Just as he finished, Aunt Phil announced it was time for bed.

While Mr. Sylvan cleared a space for them on the floor, Nate went to peer out the darkened windows. Did carrier pigeons fly at night? he wondered. Would they be able to find them here in the forest? He pressed his nose up against the thick glass, then jumped back in surprise. It was cold. Icy cold. He peered more closely. A faint dusting of ice crystals coated the window. "It's the first frost tonight," he said.

Aunt Phil straightened up from where she'd been laying out Mr. Sylvan's extra blankets. Luckily the unicorn hadn't nicked those. "That can't be right. It's been much too warm." She came over to the window, but by the time she got there, the frost had melted.

She ran her finger along the glass. "See? No frost. You probably just saw a bit of fog from your breath."

"I know the difference between fog and frost," Nate told her.

"But, Nate," she said, her voice patient, "the temperature hasn't been low enough for frost to appear. Besides, it

makes no sense for frost to appear on one window but not the others. It's easy to make mistakes when we're tired."

"I'm not tired," Nate mumbled, but Aunt Phil ignored him.

"Come along, now. We need to get some sleep. We've an early start tomorrow."

Nate sat down and took off his boots, then his jacket. He didn't like having to sleep in his shirt, but they hadn't brought nightclothes. They'd only been planning for a day trip.

As Nate settled himself on the blanket, Greasle crawled

over and curled up near his shoulder. "I don'ts likes this place," she whispered.

"Why not?" Nate asked, surprised. Of all the places he had been in the past few weeks, this one wasn't bad.

Greasle shrugged. "Too quiet. No happy sounds, like the buzz of a plane or the chug of an engine." Greasle stopped talking and cocked her left ear. "And what is that chirping sound, anyways?"

Nate held perfectly still and listened. "Crickets," he said after a moment. "Those are crickets."

Greasle shuddered. "Well, I don't like them nasty crickets."

Nate sometimes forgot that Greasle had spent her entire life burrowed inside tight, cramped engines. Things like the forest and houses were entirely foreign to her.

"It's okay. You'll be fine," Nate assured her. To cheer her up, he whispered, "Hey, look at Cornelius."

She looked over at the dodo, then squeaked in fright. "What happened to his head?"

Nate laughed softly. "That's just how he sleeps, with his head tucked under his wing like that. Doesn't it look silly? I thought it would make you laugh."

"Nothing funny about missing heads," she grumbled, then settled herself firmly in the crook of Nate's neck.

As he stared at the darkening room around them, his thoughts returned to Obediah, like a tongue probing the space where a tooth is missing. As soon as they took care of this unicorn, he had to think of a way to talk Aunt Phil into going after their black sheep of a cousin. They couldn't just wait indefinitely for him to make his next move.

The next morning, they were up with the dawn and breakfasted on soft-boiled eggs, toast, and tea. Nate was glad to hear that Cornelius would remain behind in the cottage. The dodo wasn't built for travel.

The morning was crisp, but there was no frost on the ground as Nate had feared. The sun was watery and thin, though, and its warmth barely reached down between the trees to the forest floor. They crossed a gurgling brook, where the water splashed cheerfully over moss-covered rocks. Halfway across the old stone bridge, Nate felt as if someone was watching him. His thoughts flew immediately to stories of trolls who live under bridges. He looked down at the planks of wood under his feet and tried to peer between them, but there was nothing he could see. Once they had crossed, he hung back a moment to peek beneath the bridge.

There was nothing there.

Even so, a strange chill danced across his shoulders, as if winter were drawing near. The feeling spooked him and he hurried to catch up with the others.

The trail wound upward between towering trees, then past a series of rocky ravines. The path was narrow, and looking down made Nate dizzy. He was glad when they reached the top and the terrain flattened out again. A wide, sunny meadow stretched out for nearly as far as the eye could see. Off to the right was a thick copse of trees. Once again, Nate felt he was being watched. Just as he turned to Aunt Phil to ask her if she noticed anything, he felt a faint rumbling beneath his feet.

The noise grew louder. Nate realized it was coming from

the woods. He whirled around in time to see a large white animal charge out of the trees.

It seemed easily as big as a horse, its eyes wide with fury and its teeth bared in challenge. The enormous cloven hooves tore up the ground as the unicorn thundered toward them, its long horn pointing straight at them like a spear.

Chapter Seven

Greasle screamed and Nate felt the icy-hot taste of fear on the back of his tongue.

"Mr. Sylvan!" Aunt Phil called out crisply.

The faun darted in front of them and Nate remembered his claim that the unicorn tolerated fauns better than people. He also remembered Mr. Sylvan's claim that Luminessa had been more aggressive lately.

And she was still barreling toward them.

The faun crouched low, pushed up his sleeves, and flexed his hands. Just as Nate realized Mr. Sylvan was going to try to wrestle the unicorn to a halt, the unicorn tilted her head slightly and checked her stride. She churned to a stop two feet in front of them. Before anyone could react, she knelt and lay her sharp horn on the ground at Greasle's feet.

For a long moment, no one moved, except Greasle, who was trembling with fear. "Helps?" she whispered.

Aunt Phil and Mr. Sylvan exchanged a glance. "Fascinating," Aunt Phil murmured.

Mr. Sylvan scratched his head. "I thought your little creature was some sort of monkey, not a fair maiden."

"She's a gremlin, actually, but also, apparently, a fair maid. At least as far as the unicorn is concerned. Which will make everything much easier."

"Um, could we talk about this later and help Greasle out, here?" Nate asked.

"We don't need to, Nate. The unicorn has laid her horn at Greasle's feet, a sign that she has agreed to be tamed for Greasle's sake."

"Tamed?"

"Unicorns will sometimes submit willingly to young maidens. Which," she added dryly, "it appears your gremlin is."

"You mean it won't eats me?" Greasle squeaked.

"No," Aunt Phil said. "In fact, she wants you to give her permission to rise."

At that exact moment, the unicorn's long tongue shot out and licked the gremlin in one long slurp from her ankles to the tips of her pointed ears. "Yee-uck!" Greasle said, wiping at her face. "You can gets up, you big oaf."

Gracefully, the unicorn rose to her feet. Now that Nate wasn't in fear for his life, he could see that the unicorn was actually a little smaller than a horse, about the size of a large stag. Her coat was pure white, like the foam on top of the waves. Her mane and tail were also white, but there were hints of pale gray on her muzzle and feet, as if she had waded through a pool of silver and dipped her nose to drink. She smelled faintly of ripening apples.

Aunt Phil leaned forward and blew into the unicorn's nostrils. The unicorn whuffled and shook her head.

"Greetings, Luminessa, daughter of Fleetfoot and Wonder. It has been too long since we've exchanged breath." Still holding the unicorn's gaze with her own, Aunt Phil slowly put her hand out and laid it on the unicorn's horn.

"As a male, you can never do this unless there is a maiden nearby to tame her," she told Nate in a low voice.

The unicorn snorted and whoofed. Aunt Phil nodded, as if she understood perfectly. "I'd like you to meet my nephew, Nathaniel Fludd. He's the current beastologist-in-training." To Nate she said, "Here. Come blow in her face so she can smell you, then put your hand on her horn right beneath mine."

Nate hesitated. It seemed kind of rude to just go up and blow in someone's face. Seeing him hang back, Aunt Phil said, "Don't worry. Not only is it how they greet one another, it's how they identify us. Once you've exchanged breath with a unicorn, the chances are very high it will never attack you unprovoked."

"Just don't let her lick you," Greasle muttered darkly.

Nate stepped forward, tilted his head a bit so that he was closer to the unicorn's nostrils, then huffed out a soft puff of breath. Next, he placed his hand on the horn, surprised at how warm and smooth it was.

This time when Luminessa made the snorting and whuffling sounds, he *felt* them, a rumbling deep in his chest, as

if he himself were speaking words without actually moving his mouth. Much to his shock, he could feel what the words were as they formed in his chest.

He is but a colt, the unicorn was saying.

"We all have to start sometime," Aunt Phil said. "Besides, you are barely older than a colt yourself."

The unicorn snorted again. *In unicorn years, which are much different from your human years.*

"True enough," Aunt Phil said.

"What are unicorn years?" Nate asked.

"For every human year that passes, unicorns only age six

months. They often live well into their hundreds, which is more than two hundred years of age in human years."

Nate felt a tug on his sleeve and looked down.

"Does gremlins have gremlin years?" Greasle whispered.

"I don't know," Nate told her. Before he could ask, Aunt Phil spoke to the unicorn again. "Mr. Sylvan says you've been feeling poorly. I thought you should have an examination."

Hmm, rumbled deep in Nate's chest. *Certainly feel different. Strange, even. I think I would like an examination, please.* She stopped talking and cocked her head to the side, her nostrils quivering. Her head swung back in Greasle's direction. Then she reached out with her long pink tongue and licked the gremlin from toe to head again.

Greasle squealed, and the unicorn gave a small hum of pleasure. *Rich and salty,* Nate felt deep in his chest.

"Horse spit," Greasle said disgustedly, wiping her face with her hand.

"Unicorn saliva, to be precise," Aunt Phil said absentmindedly. She looked from Luminessa back to Greasle, a thoughtful expression on her face.

"What?" Nate asked.

"I'm wondering if her appetite for Greasle is a symptom of her illness. Like a dog who eats grass to soothe his stomach, or how sometimes people eat dirt to add iron or minerals to their diet."

Nate looked from Greasle to the unicorn. "Do you think Luminessa is low on grease? Or oil?"

"It's a possibility."

The unicorn swished her tufted tail and began heading back toward the trees. "We'll be back shortly," Aunt Phil told Mr. Sylvan. "Greasle, would you mind coming with us? Your presence will make everything easier."

"Hmph," Greasle grumbled. "If she promises to stop sliming me."

"Nonsense," Aunt Phil said. "This is the cleanest you've been in weeks."

Greasle opened her mouth to disagree, but Nate picked her up and brought her close. "Don't argue! Maybe this will help convince her to let me keep you."

Greasle's face brightened. "You thinks so?"

Nate shrugged. "She seems pretty happy with your effect on the unicorn."

Greasle sighed. "Okay, then."

The unicorn led them deep into a tangle of woods, where the branches were thick and nearly impenetrable in some places. Nate could hear the bubbling of a small brook nearby. A large, jagged rock rose up in front of them, taller than a house. As the unicorn disappeared behind it, Nate scrambled after her, then stopped and sucked in his breath at the scene before him.

A small grassy area was covered with delicate branches. They had become interwoven as they'd grown and now formed a small bower, a little cave. The bower backed up to a sheer drop on either side. The only way in or out was the way they had come. Crowded against the back of the small space was a pile of rags: a tablecloth, a pair of tea towels, pillow fluff, and, Nate thought, a small patch of goat hide.

"This will be perfect," Aunt Phil said, kneeling on the ground. Nate knelt beside her while the unicorn nimbly lowered herself into the small nest she'd built.

"Greasle, dear, I'll need you to sit right here by her head where she can see you and smell you," Aunt Phil directed.

Greasle's eyes widened at the word *dear*, and Nate gave her an encouraging nod. Surely that could only be a good sign.

Aunt Phil pulled her medical bag closer. "If you'd lie on your right side, please," she instructed the unicorn. She opened her bag and rummaged around inside until she produced a thermometer. A rather large thermometer, Nate realized.

"Open wide," she said.

Luminessa delicately pulled back her lips. "This goes

under your tongue," Aunt Phil said, "but no matter what you do, don't bite down on it."

The unicorn rested her teeth gingerly on the glass of the thermometer, her eyes nearly crossing as she looked at it.

"Pet her," Aunt Phil told the gremlin. "It will help her keep calm."

Greasle's eyes grew wide with fear.

"I can pet her," Nate offered, scooting forward.

"No. You're not a maiden, Nate. She'll tolerate your presence now that she knows your breath, but only a maiden is able to calm her."

Greasle rolled her eyes. "The big baby," she muttered. Tentatively, she reached toward the unicorn. She lifted one tiny finger and cautiously ran it down the side of the unicorn's neck. The skin there shimmied and rippled, and the unicorn visibly relaxed.

"Excellent!" Aunt Phil said, and Greasle's cheeks grew pink with pleasure.

Aunt Phil pulled the thermometer out of Luminessa's mouth, and Nate nearly laughed as the unicorn's lips twitched and wiggled. "Let me show you how to read this. See these lines, and the numbers next to them? And that thick silver line in the middle? Where does it stop?"

"One hundred and ten?"

"Exactly. One hundred and ten. A horse's normal temperature runs between ninety-nine and one hundred and two. A unicorn's is slightly higher, in the area of one hundred and five to one hundred and six. This is elevated, even for a unicorn."

"So she has a fever?"

"Yes." Aunt Phil's face was shadowed with worry as she cleaned off the thermometer and returned it to her pack. "Stick out your tongue, please."

Luminessa did as she was told. Aunt Phil ran her fingers along the creature's gums and checked the color of her tongue. "A little darker than normal, I think." She frowned in concern. "Hoof, please," she said cheerfully, but Nate wasn't fooled. He didn't think the unicorn was, either.

Luminessa lifted one dainty hoof. Aunt Phil gently prodded it. "A tiny bit of swelling, I see." She placed the unicorn's foot back on the grass, then turned to her bag.

The unicorn snorted and whuffled. Still rummaging through her things, Aunt Phil said, "See what she's trying to say, Nate."

"Me?" he squeaked.

"Yes, you."

Eyeing the sharp horn, Nate swallowed nervously, then scooted closer. He glanced at Greasle. "Keep petting her," he said.

The gremlin redoubled her petting efforts.

Nate slowly put his hand on Luminessa's smooth horn. "Um, could you repeat that, please?"

Does she know what is wrong?

Nate could hear a note of alarm in the unicorn's voice. "She's wondering if you know what's wrong with her," he told Aunt Phil.

"I will in just one more minute," Aunt Phil said. "Aha, there it is," she said, and pulled a long stethoscope from her bag. She first positioned the two earpieces, then placed the round, flat disk on the unicorn's chest. "Hmmm," she muttered, still frowning. She moved the disk to a new location. "Hmmm." She pursed her lips and motioned Nate closer. "Here." She snapped the stethoscope in place on his ears. "Tell me what you hear."

She placed the disk back on Luminessa's chest. Nate listened carefully. And then he heard it. A faint thu-*bump,*

thu-*bump*. "It's her heartbeat!" he said. If there was some-thing wrong with her heart, *that* could be serious.

"Very good. Now listen more closely. Hold your own breath if you have to."

Nate did as he was told. Thu-*bump*-*bump*. Thu-*bump*-*bump*. He looked at Aunt Phil, puzzled. "It's almost as if there are two hearts beating."

A slow smile spread across Aunt Phil's face. "Precisely." She turned to the unicorn. "My dear, you are fine. Indeed, you are more than fine. You are foaling."

"Foaling?" Nate asked blankly.

"Foaling. It means she's going to have a baby."

Nate's hand was still on the unicorn's horn, so he heard her joyful *I am?* Was it his imagination or was there a faint blush of pink on her white cheeks?

"You are," Aunt Phil said. "And may I be the first to con-gratulate you, my dear. This is a very, very special occasion. Let's get you comfortable, and then I'll return tomorrow with a few things you'll need."

A baby . . . Nate felt Luminessa's hum of pleasure all the way down to his toes. Not wanting to eavesdrop on a pri-vate moment, he quickly let go of her horn.

"Can I stops petting her now?" Greasle asked.

"Yes, you can. And thank you for your help." Aunt Phil put all her things back in her pack and pushed to her feet. Nate stood up and brushed the bracken off his knees.

Aunt Phil bade the unicorn farewell and repeated her promise to return in the morning. She smiled the entire way back to the clearing. "Well," she announced to Mr. Sylvan. "I have the answer to your great unicorn mystery."

"What is it, then?" he asked, getting to his hooves and brushing off his hindquarters.

"She's foaling."

"Foaling?" he repeated, his eyes nearly goggling out of his head. "You mean she's going to have a young'un?"

Aunt Phil beamed. "Yes. Which explains why you didn't recognize the symptoms."

"Aye," the faun said, scratching his head behind one of his horns. "How long has it been since there's been a babe? I've been a caretaker for nearly thirty years and I've never seen it."

"This is the first time in more than forty years we've had such an occasion. In fact, the last unicorn of record to give birth was Luminessa's mother."

"Forty years?" Nate repeated. "I thought you said she was a young unicorn."

"She is, Nate. In unicorn years she's only half that and has just entered adulthood. In all the time I've been a beastologist, this is only the second unicorn foal I've heard of." Aunt Phil turned back to Mr. Sylvan. "We'll have to alter her care a bit. When we get back to the cabin, I'll write you up a list of new instructions and make up a special mash for her."

Aunt Phil and Mr. Sylvan started back down the path to his house, heads close together as they talked about the unicorn's care. Nate turned for one last look over his shoulder at the path that led to the unicorn's bower. It was so well protected, you'd never even know it was there. Both the mother and baby should be well hidden from any predators or other intruders.

He turned back around and hurried to catch up to Aunt Phil, his feet crunching faintly over a thin layer of ice. He thought about mentioning it to Aunt Phil to prove he hadn't been wrong about last night's frost, but decided he didn't want to poke a hole in her good mood.

Chapter Eight

WHEN THEY RETURNED TO THE COTTAGE, Cornelius came waddling out to meet them. "Well?" he asked.

Aunt Phil bent down, grasped the dodo under his wings, picked him up, and twirled him around. Cornelius gave a little squawk of surprise. "She's foaling, Cornelius! She's going to have a baby! In our lifetime, no less!" Aunt Phil set the dodo back down and beamed at him.

Nate smiled. He had never see Aunt Phil giddy like this.

"Well," said the dodo, adjusting his feathers. "That *is* good news."

"It's wonderful news! Let's see. We'll need more blankets, and vitamin tonic, and extra apples, and an oat mash . . . oh, and we should try to find her some quince. Unicorns are quite partial to quince, and since she is foaling, she could do with a few luxuries." Aunt Phil paused in making her list. "I think she's quite far along, but I'll have to check Justina Fludd's writings on the subject." She turned to Mr. Sylvan. "Have you seen any other unicorns here in Broceliande?"

The faun shook his head. "Not a one. And with her acting so strangely and all, you can be certain I've been looking."

"Is she the only unicorn in the forest?" Nate asked.

"The only one. All unicorns have their own territory. They are such solitary creatures that even another unicorn is too much company for them." She ruffled his hair and smiled at him. "Except when they're foaling, of course. They will share their forest with their own offspring."

Nate tried to smile back, but thinking about foaling made him think about families, and *that* made him miss his own family. But he didn't want to spoil Aunt Phil's happiness. "I think I'll go read up on unicorns, if you don't mind," he said.

"That's an excellent idea, Nate."

He and Greasle retired to the living room, where he carefully lifted the ancient, worn copy of *The Book of Beasts* from Aunt Phil's pack, then stretched out in front of the fire. There was a tiny grunt as Greasle came and stretched out next to him, propping her chin in her hands. "You lookin' up unicorns?"

"Yep."

"Check and see if it says anything about their spit," she said, wiping at her face.

He hid a smile and, scooting the book closer to her, began to turn the pages. It was easy to forget what he was looking for as he thumbed through the book. Tantalizing pictures of strange beasts, both beautiful and terrifying, covered its pages. *Basilisks, Bonnacons, Centaurs, Chimeras, Dragons, Griffins, Hippocampus, Kraakens, Manticores . . .*

"Hey!" Greasle said, sitting up with a scowl. "Does it say anything about dodos in there?"

Nate put his finger on the page to hold his place, then thumbed back through the book. "Nope. No dodos."

"Ha!" Greasle said. "And he thinks he's so special." Smiling contentedly, she snuggled back down.

Nate went back to the book. *Selkies, Trolls, Uldras, Unicorns . . .*

There it was! Right after *Uldras* and just before *Wyverns.* He began to read:

Unicornis europus

Also known as the Western unicorn, this creature is the size of a large stag or a horse, white in color, with a tufted tail, cloven hooves, and a horn two cubits long protruding from its brow. The <u>Unicornis europus</u> also includes the German eichorn, which has a shaggier mane and coarser coat and whose horn has slightly raised ridges.

It is said that the unicorn is so ferocious it cannot be taken alive. This, however, is not true. Justina Fludd, beloved young daughter of Sir Mungo Fludd, was the first to capture a unicorn without injury. No one was more surprised than she when the wild creature walked up to her, gentle as a lamb, and laid its head in her lap. Unfortunately, many unscrupulous hunters quickly learned of this weakness, many a poor maiden was tricked into luring unicorns to greedy hunters.

Nate spent the rest of the evening drawing and trying not to think about his parents or Obediah. He

fell asleep next to Greasle, with visions of ferocious uni-corns and evil hunters prancing through his head.

Early the next morning, Aunt Phil, Nate, Greasle, and Mr. Sylvan left for the unicorn's bower just as the first rays of sunlight filtered down through the trees. It had grown even colder during the night and Nate had to stomp his feet to keep them warm.

On the way up to the meadow, Nate kept a careful lookout for carrier pigeons. Now that they knew there was nothing seriously wrong with Luminessa, it was time to turn their attention back to the problem of Obediah. Surely he wasn't going to disappear forever. He'd pretty much promised they'd hear from him again.

Nate's greatest fear was that they'd miss that message. Unable to locate either his parents' lawyer or Miss Lumpton, his former governess, Nate knew Obediah was the only possible link to his missing family.

Mr. Sylvan decided to wait for them in the meadow, even though the unicorn wasn't having a personal examination that morning. Something about needing to maintain territories and boundaries. They left him lying in the grass, staring up at the fluffy white clouds, playing his reed pipes.

They found Luminessa waiting for them just outside her bower. When she saw Greasle, she pranced excitedly and dipped her horn up and down a few times, then whinnied.

"Go on." Aunt Phil nudged the gremlin forward. "She's eager to see you."

"Oh, brother," Greasle muttered. She put her hands on her hips and glared at the unicorn. "But no licking!"

Once the unicorn had sniffed Greasle all over (and sneaked in one loud slurp), Aunt Phil settled down to the business of giving her some instructions.

"You're to have a spoonful of this each day. Mr. Sylvan will come up to administer it and you must let him, do you understand me?"

Luminessa nodded.

"And no sneaking any nips of his hide, either. If you need extra fluffing, we've brought you two more blankets and a pillow."

The unicorn whuffled and snorted.

"See what she's saying, Nate. It's good practice for you."

Nate put his hand on her horn and asked her to repeat what she'd just said. *When will the baby arrive?* Luminessa asked. Nate repeated the question for Aunt Phil.

"Sooner rather than later, I think," Aunt Phil said. "But it happens so rarely that I'm not as up on unicorn pregnancy as I should be. I will research the matter as soon as we get home and should have an answer when we return in a week."

Luminessa was sad to see Greasle go and consoled herself by shredding the pillow and blankets into nesting fluff.

Feeling kindly toward the unicorn now that she was no longer keeping them from the matter of Obediah, Nate wished her good luck, then followed Aunt Phil back toward the meadow. He had to hurry to catch up to her—she was so happy, she was practically skipping.

Nate skipped, too, but not because of the unicorn. He skipped because he was eager to get back to hunting for information about his parents.

When Aunt Phil saw that he was struggling to keep up with her, she slowed down and gave him a sheepish smile. "I'm sorry. It's just so rare in our field to have such good news," she said. "We're often dealing with illness or injuries or the stupidity of man. But this, well, this is one of those rare moments that erase all the hard work and disappointments." She smiled at him, and he smiled back. They were still smiling when they reached the meadow.

"Mr. Sylvan! We're done," Nate called out. He hurried around the last tree blocking the path into the clearing, then stumbled to a halt. Mr. Sylvan sat on a boulder with his hands and feet bound by rope and a gag stuffed into his mouth. He struggled against the restraints, making squeaking noises and motioning with his head.

Before Nate could react or call out a warning, a barrel-shaped figure with ginger hair stepped out from behind the trees next to the boulder. Nate's jaw dropped open and a sick feeling flooded his stomach. Behind him, he felt Aunt Phil stiffen.

"Hello, cousins," Obediah Fludd said. "Long time no see, eh?"

Chapter Nine

NATE BLINKED TWICE. He'd been wanting desperately to find Obediah, but now, faced with the slippery, dishonest man, he felt ill.

"How very thoughtful of you to lead me straight to the unicorn. You've saved me a great deal of trouble, you know. I was so wanting a unicorn horn of my own—the promise of long life, you see—and you've brought me straight to it! I didn't have to break into anyone's house to steal a map this time. All I had to do was follow you."

Aunt Phil looked thunderstruck. "B-but how? Mr. Sylvan, at least, should have been able to sense you, even if I couldn't."

"Oh, I didn't follow you myself! Oh dear, no. Much too risky. I had Frozndorf here do it."

For the first time, Nate noticed a stocky little man standing in Obediah's shadow. He was quite short, only coming up to Obediah's hip. He looked a lot like a small dwarf out of a fairy tale, with leathery skin and long white hair that reached well past his back. He was dressed all in dingy white, from his trousers to his fur cape. He looked uncomfortably hot, and sweat was dripping off his face. Where it hit the ground, small patches of frost formed. The grass under his feet was frozen and stiff with ice.

"An uldra!" Aunt Phil said. "This far south! Are you insane? The poor thing will catch his death in this climate. It's much too warm for him."

Obediah waved his hand dismissively. "He lives to serve me, don't you, Frozndorf?"

Frozndorf cringed and wrung his hands, then looked down at his feet. "Yes, master," he said, his words bringing a chill breeze into the air of the meadow.

Seeing the pitiful uldra seemed to restore Aunt Phil's spirits. "What do you want from us?" she asked.

"Why, many things, dear cousin. Mostly, I want wealth and fame and recognition, the sort you and your side of the family have received for centuries."

"Well, you'll have to do more than follow in my footsteps and harass the beasts. You'll need to work for those things."

"Oh, I think not. I find that working is so overrated. Your side of the family may have done things the hard way, but I assure you that I do not intend to go that route. I have another plan in mind." Obediah rubbed his hands together.

Aunt Phil strode over to Obediah and leaned forward so that

they were practically nose to nose. "You will not touch a single hair on that unicorn, do you hear me? Not. One. Hair."

He smiled, unaffected by her temper. "And who will stop me this time? You have no ferocious dragons to call upon to enforce your demands. No, dear cousin, I think you are a bit out of luck on this one." He looked down to examine his hand, then polished his fingernails on his jacket. "However, if you are willing to make a trade, we might have something to talk about."

"Trade? Trade what?"

"I will leave the unicorn be, if you will give me *The Book of Beasts*."

"You are out of your mind!" Aunt Phil exclaimed. "Hand you the secret locations of every one of the world's most rare and wondrous beasts? I think not."

"Not even to save the unicorn? You know what I will need to do to get that horn."

Aunt Phil's face turned deathly white. *Kill her,* thought Nate. *He has to kill her to get the horn.* Nate glared at Obediah, hatred roiling in his gut.

"You're asking me to condemn all the other beasts to death in order to save this one. I can't do that."

"You don't know that I want them all dead," Obediah pointed out.

"I don't know that you *don't*. What do you want them for, anyway?"

He smiled again, an oily thing that reminded Nate of an eel. "Ah, ah, ah! That would be telling. You'll just have to wait and see along with the rest of the world." His smile disappeared and his face became twisted with bitterness and hate. "Now hand it over."

"I will not hand over *The Book of Beasts*. And you will have to get through me to get to the unicorn. So give it your best shot."

Instead of getting mad, Obediah smiled again. Something in his expression made Nate feel as if a cold snake were slithering around inside his stomach. "Oh, I think you'll give me what I want."

"You're daft if you think that."

"Really? You won't give me *The Book of Beasts*? Not even if I promise to tell you where the boy's parents are?"

Chapter Ten

ALL OF THE AIR WHOOSHED OUT of Nate's lungs, and black spots danced in front of his eyes. They were quickly replaced with a haze of red fury. Without even thinking, Nate launched himself at Obediah, only to have Aunt Phil grasp him firmly by the collar. "Steady, Nate," she said in a low voice. Then, louder, she asked, "Are they alive?"

"Yes. And quite ready to come home, if only you'll give me the book. I'm sure they won't understand that a handful of beasts are more important to you than they are. I know the boy won't."

"Do you have proof?"

Still smiling, Obediah reached into his waistcoat and pulled something from an inside pocket. He held it out to Aunt Phil.

Glaring at him, she took what he offered. Nate stepped closer so he could see.

It was a photograph. Of his parents. There was a wrecked airship in the background, with pieces and debris strewn onto the ice behind them. They sat, huddled together for warmth, wrapped in blankets and furs. Nate's heart leaped so high, it nearly flew out of his chest. They *were* alive! He knew it! Nate looked up at Aunt Phil.

"How do you come to have this?" she asked. "And if they're still alive, why have they been declared dead?"

Obediah spread his hands wide. "Spitsbergen is very close to my territory, cousin, so you can be sure that I take a great interest in any exploration that goes on in that area.

"Imagine my joy at discovering that my very own flesh and blood were onboard that historic flight! When news of the crash arrived"—he clucked his tongue and shook his head—"of course I had to offer any assistance I could."

Aunt Phil snorted. "You hurried forward hoping you could get your hands on Horatio's copy of *The Geographica*, you mean."

Obediah smiled again. "Really, this suspicious streak of yours is most unbecoming. Because of my extensive knowledge of the area and my local contacts, I reached the boy's parents well before the official rescue party and offered them my hospitality."

Alive, alive, Nate's heart kept singing. *His parents were alive!*

"How do we know nothing has happened to them since this photograph was taken?" she asked.

Obediah shrugged. "You don't. But there needs to be

trust between cousins, don't you think? You'll simply have to take my word for it."

"Where are you holding them?"

"Close enough that once the book is in my possession, I have only to send a message and they will be released immediately. They should arrive at Batting-at-the-Flies in

a matter of hours." He thrust his big hand forward and wiggled his fingers greedily.

Aunt Phil stared at his hand for a long moment while Nate held his breath. What was she waiting for, anyway?

"You don't think I have it on me, do you?" she said at last. Nate barely managed to keep from gasping at the lie.

"Surely you understand that I don't carry something as valuable as that around with me?" Aunt Phil said.

Nate scowled at her, and she gave an almost imperceptible shake of her head. Nate seethed inside. What she was up to?

"How do *you* know where to find the beasts, then?" Obediah asked, clearly suspicious.

"How did *you*?" Aunt Phil asked. "How were you able to locate the phoenix and the basilisk and the wyverns without *The Book of Beasts*?"

Obediah smiled. "Oh, that was clever of me, wasn't it? I borrowed—*stole* is such an ugly word, don't you think?—a couple of maps of Africa when I visited the boy's home. I came upon a map of Dinas Emrys when I was, er, visiting your house."

Nate frowned. "Wait. You didn't search my house until after you returned from Africa."

Obediah gave an unpleasant smile. "That was the *second* time I'd visited your house, boy," he said. "The first time, I stopped by and had tea with your nanny. What was her name? Miss Lumpton, I believe. She and I had a lovely visit. I'm afraid you were upstairs, sick with the mumps, so I didn't get a chance to meet you that time. She was kind enough to give me a tour of your father's study and work-room. She was such a dull old thing. It was easy enough to sneak a map or two when she was bleating on about how worried she was and wondering what would happen to her when you finally went to join your parents. Now, enough chatting. Hand over the book."

"I told you, I don't have it. I've been a practicing beast-ologist for well over forty years. I have all the beasts' loca-tions memorized at this point."

Nate wondered if Obediah would know she was lying. He'd searched her house himself and not found it. Would he go along with her claim?

Obediah weighed her words. "Very well. I will give you forty-eight hours. That should be enough time to get back to Batting-at-the-Flies, then return here to Broceliande. If you do not return to this exact spot with *The Book of Beasts* by then, I will take what I need from the unicorn and you will never find the boy's parents. No one will ever find them. Alive."

Chapter Eleven

POINTING OUT THAT FAUNS WERE OF NO VALUE TO HIM, Obediah let Aunt Phil untie Mr. Sylvan so he could return to the cottage with them.

As soon as they stepped out of the clearing, Nate turned to Aunt Phil. "Why didn't you give—"

"Shh!" She reached out lightning fast and clamped a hand over his mouth, surprising him. "Voices carry. And who knows whether or nor that poor little uldra is following us. Say nothing until I tell you it is safe. Do you understand?"

With her hand still clamped firmly over his mouth, Nate nodded. Aunt Phil removed her hand and looked solemnly at the gremlin huddling on Nate's shoulder. "Greasle, dear. I have an enormous favor to ask of you."

Greasle stepped a little closer to Nate's neck. "I don't likes the sound of that," she whispered.

Aunt Phil took a deep breath. "Having Obediah so near the unicorn is a disaster waiting to happen. If Luminessa gets wind of him, she might get violent and try to do him serious injury. Or kill him."

"Seems to me that would be a good thing," Greasle said.

"With Obediah dead, we would have no way of learning anything further about Nate's parents. Greasle, only you can keep Luminessa properly calm until this ugly dance has played itself out. Could you—*would* you—please stay with her until Nate and I can return with a way out of this mess?"

Nate heard a little gulp right by his ear. "All by myselfs?" Greasle asked in a small voice.

"Yes, I'm afraid only you are small enough to go undetected by Obediah. I'm also hoping that your scent will be so unfamiliar to the uldra that he won't realize you are even there."

Greasle's eyes grew huge. She looked up at Nate. "Does I have to?"

Nate was torn. He didn't want to put the gremlin in any danger, but they didn't dare risk a showdown between Obediah and the unicorn. At least not until he'd freed Nate's parents.

"No," Aunt Phil answered. "You don't have to."

Nate felt Greasle relax slightly.

"But if you do," Aunt Phil continued, "you will earn a place in our household for as long as you'd like."

Greasle's ears poked up. "You means it?"

"I mean it. You can stay with Nate as long as you want."

Greasle groaned and put her hands on either side of her head, as if she were in pain.

"I'm sorry," Aunt Phil said. "I know I'm asking a lot, but I don't have any other choice."

Greasle looked up at Nate. "Should I do it?"

Nate looked down into her little scrunched face. "I think this is a decision you have to make," he said.

Greasle turned back to Aunt Phil. "Is that nasty mans really going to hurt that slobber-tongued horse?"

"He easily could. Especially if she gets frightened and

threatens him in any way. But with you, a young maid, around, she will remain calm."

"And I'll get to stay with Nate forever?"

"Forever."

Greasle's face wrinkled as she thought long and hard. Finally she said, "Okay, I'll do it," and Nate breathed a huge sigh of relief.

"That's our gremlin!" Aunt Phil said. "Can you find your way back there or do you need me to give you directions?"

Greasle studied the trees. "It's thattaways." She pointed in the exact direction of the bower.

"Excellent. Get yourself over there and tell Luminessa what's happened. And keep her calm, at all costs."

Greasle gave a snappy salute, then jumped from Nate's shoulder to the ground. "Don't takes too long," she told them.

"We won't," Nate promised, then watched as she disappeared into the trees.

It was a long, tense walk back to Mr. Sylvan's cabin. Nate seethed with ugly thoughts and angry questions the whole way. Every single thing he loved or cared about seemed to hang in the balance: his parents, Greasle, even his future as a beastologist.

Once they reached the cottage and went inside, Nate rounded on Aunt Phil. "I told you I saw frost," he reminded her. "I told you." That wasn't what he had planned to say at all. He'd wanted to shout, *Why didn't you give him the stupid book? What are we going to do about my parents?* But that was what had come out.

"You did, Nate."

Her agreeing didn't make him any less angry. "You should have listened to me." He wasn't sure what exactly he wanted from her. An admission, an apology, *something*.

"What? What happened?" Cornelius asked, looking from one angry face to the other.

"Obediah," Aunt Phil said shortly. "I'm afraid he followed us to the unicorn's bower."

The dodo made a whistling sound and threw Mr. Sylvan a withering look. "A fine caretaker you turned out to be." He sniffed. "I thought that was the whole point of having a faun do the caretaking—their ability to sense changes or disturbances in the forest."

"Obediah had an uldra do the actual following," Aunt Phil explained. "An uldra's scent isn't known to the fauns, and even if it was, the chill an uldra produces deadens the sense of smell."

"So what does that black sheep of a Fludd want?"

"*The Book of Beasts.* He'll trade the unicorn for it." She glanced at Nate. "Along with Nate's parents."

"What?" squawked Cornelius.

As Aunt Phil explained exactly what had happened,

Nate went over to the window. He was so restless, so eager to do something, that he was afraid he'd explode. And he missed Greasle already. Her small jokes and grumbles, the way she tried to make him feel better about things. It was as if he'd left a piece of himself back there.

His misery ignited into anger. He folded his arms and glared at Aunt Phil. "If you'd trusted me, listened to me, then you would have known something was wrong. Instead, you acted as if I was just making things up and being a dumb little kid." His voice trembled with all the things he wanted to shout at her.

Aunt Phil ran her hand through her hair, mussing it. "I know. It was wrong of me. I'm sorry. I was preoccupied with the unicorn, and wondering where Obediah would strike next, and worried that you were giving yourself false hope about your parents."

"But I was right about them," Nate whispered.

Aunt Phil's face twisted with regret. "You were."

Then Nate dropped his gaze and stared down at his toes. "Why didn't you give him the book?" he asked in an even tinier whisper.

"Oh, Nate!" Aunt Phil threw her arms around him and

hugged him close. Part of him longed for the comfort she offered, but he was too angry with her to accept it. He wriggled out of her grasp. "Why?"

Aunt Phil sighed and sat back on her heels. "I can't, Nate. It is my sworn duty to protect *The Book of Beasts*, and the animals it contains, with my life."

"But my parents!" he said, his voice rising.

"Do you know just how many Fludds have given their lives to protect that book, those beasts? If I hand it over, all their sacrifices will have been for nothing. I can't do that, Nate. We'll think of something else, some other way to get your parents back and keep the unicorn safe. I just need a little time to come up with an idea. Now, come on. Let's pack up our things and get back to the house. I want to put some feelers out among my contacts. If your parents are truly only hours away from Batting-at-the-Flies, one of my contacts should know. I find it hard to believe that Obediah has managed to fool us all."

The plane ride from France took forever. Nate was so agitated, he could barely sit still. Cornelius kept giving him dirty looks and finally got so frustrated with Nate's squirming that he snapped at him with his huge, heavy beak.

"Sit *still!*" he complained. "You're crimping my tail feathers."

Nate glanced at Aunt Phil up in the cockpit. Between the roar of the engine and the rushing wind, she couldn't hear a thing. "I don't care about your stupid tail feathers," he told Cornelius. "Why do you even need feathers, anyway? You can't fly. Except in a plane."

The dodo lunged forward and snapped at Nate again, this time catching his forearm.

"Ow!" Nate narrowed his eyes, then reached over and plucked out one of the dodo's tail feathers.

Cornelius gave a squawk of protest and snatched for the feather with his beak. Nate held it out over the edge of the cockpit, then let it go.

The dodo's mouth opened in surprise, then clacked shut. "My feather!" he wailed.

Immediately, Nate was filled with remorse, but he

couldn't bring himself to apologize. "You bit me," he pointed out.

Cornelius whipped his hind end around and backed up so that his rump was squashed against the front of the cockpit, safely out of Nate's reach. They ignored each other for the rest of the trip, and Nate couldn't help but wonder if Cornelius would tell on him. He was sure that yanking tail feathers was something a true beastologist would never do.

Chapter Twelve

Aunt Phil landed just as the sun was setting. They'd cut the timing close, as there was barely enough daylight to bring the plane in. As soon as it touched down, Nate scrambled out of the cockpit and waited impatiently for Aunt Phil to dismount.

"So what's your plan?" he asked.

She took off her leather helmet and looked around. "Where's Cornelius?"

"He's still in the plane."

She went over to the plane and lugged the dodo out of

the cockpit with a grunt. Nate held his breath, wondering if the bird would tell on him, relieved when Cornelius contented himself with sending Nate a withering glare.

"So what's your plan?" Nate repeated as they headed to the house.

Aunt Phil ran her hand through her hair. "I haven't got one yet, Nate. I'm still thinking."

"But we're running out of time!" he said.

"We've still got a good forty hours left. First we need to get some food, then some rest so we can think clearly."

Nate grumbled, but Aunt Phil didn't budge. After setting her things down in the hall, she headed for the kitchen and lit the stove. He followed and sat at the kitchen table, watching her, willing her to think of some brilliant plan that would bring his parents home safely.

It was a silent dinner of sardines on toast. Even Cornelius didn't say much. When they'd finished, Aunt Phil sent Nate up to bed. There was no way he would be able to sleep, but he didn't bother to argue. As he clomped up the stairs to his room, he heard her shouting into the telephone. "Check with the selkies. If Nate's parents came from the north, the selkies might have seen them. And the barnacle geese.

They're nosy busybodies. If anyone matching Horatio or Adele Fludd's description came their way, they'll have noticed."

Once in his room, Nate found he missed Greasle even more. The room, which had begun to feel familiar, now just felt empty. Prisonlike. He threw himself on the bed and stared at the ceiling.

He wanted to do something. Something that would allow him to get his parents back. He needed a plan.

He sat bolt upright as an idea crashed into his head. It was so simple, he was surprised he hadn't thought of it before. He'd get *The Book of Beasts* and take it to Obediah himself. Once his parents were free, then they could all work on getting the book back so Obediah couldn't find any more beasts.

Nate swung his legs off the bed. Aunt Phil might think the beasts were more important than his parents, but he didn't. He hadn't sworn any dumb oath, either.

He tiptoed to the door and opened it a crack. The hall was dark and silent. Aunt Phil's bedroom was all the way down at the end. Did she keep *The Book of Beasts* in there with her at night? She might, so he would try there first.

Nate crept silently down the hall until he came to her room. He put his ear to the closed door but heard nothing—no snoring, no rustling of covers. If Aunt Phil was in there, she was being awfully quiet.

He placed his hand on the knob and turned it oh-so-gently, ready to stop if it gave so much as a squeak. Then he slowly pushed the door open.

The room was dark, so it took his eyes a moment to adjust. When they did, he saw that Aunt Phil's bed was empty. In fact, it didn't look as if she'd even been up there yet.

He tried to work up his courage to actually search through her things, but he couldn't. Instead, he tiptoed back out and closed the door behind him, then headed for the stairway. He did his best to stay close to the banister, where the stairs creaked the least. He paused on the bottom step. While he debated whether the book would be in the kitchen or her study, he heard the murmur of voices. He strained to hear what they were saying.

"The boy will never forgive you," Cornelius said.

"He will in time. He'll understand once he's older," was Aunt Phil's response.

"Do you really think they are still alive?" the dodo asked.

Nate held his breath as he waited for Aunt Phil's answer.

"I'm not sure," she said at last. "I certainly hope so, for Nate's sake as well as my own. But if they are, why did Obediah wait until now to make this offer? Why didn't he come forward sooner?"

"Maybe he'd hoped he wouldn't need to?" Cornelius suggested. "Maybe he thought he could do whatever he planned using only *The Geographica*?"

"Well, that's the thing. I'm not so sure he has *The Geographica*, which is partly why I worry he might not have the boy's parents. He didn't admit to having it, for one thing. If he did have it, surely he'd have gloated and rubbed my nose in it."

"Then how did he know where to find the beasts?" Cornelius asked.

"He told us he'd stolen the maps. One from me and a couple from a visit to Nate's governess. And we led him straight to the unicorn ourselves. I don't have all the answers, Corny. I just know all the pieces aren't fitting together quite right. We'll know more once my contacts begin reporting back, but I'm not particularly hopeful."

Aunt Phil's words stole all of Nate's determination right

out of him. He sat down on the bottom step. She thought Obediah was lying. She still wasn't convinced his parents were alive. He felt too discouraged to even climb back up the stairs to bed. Instead, he laid his head down on the hard wooden step and closed his eyes.

Nate woke up to the smell of frying bacon. He was stiff and achy from sleeping on the step. He noticed someone had covered him with a blanket during the night.

With a hollow, empty feeling, he realized he'd missed his chance to sneak around downstairs and steal *The Book of Beasts*. He'd never be able to pull it off in the broad light of day.

His stomach gave out a grumble, so he blinked the sleep from his eyes and followed his nose to the kitchen. "Have you thought of a plan yet?" he asked.

"Well, good morning to you, too," Cornelius drawled.

"Hush," Aunt Phil told the dodo. "No, Nate. I haven't. Have you?"

"No," he said glumly, taking a seat and planting his elbows on the table. He wasn't going to tell her about last night's plan to steal *The Book of Beasts*. "It's too bad we don't have two copies of *The Book of Beasts*," he mumbled.

"Nate!" Aunt Phil turned from the stove to stare at him. "That's it! What a brilliant idea!"

"What idea?" A tiny butterfly wing of hope fluttered in Nate's chest.

"We will make a false *Book of Beasts*! One so true to life and with maps so close to the originals that it will take Obediah months to discover the treachery."

Nate thought about it for a minute. It wasn't a bad plan, he decided. "But can you do that in the time we have left?"

"I can. If you help me." They stared at each other for a long moment, and Nate felt all sorts of unspoken things in that silence. A peace offering for one, but also a plea for understanding, a hope that somehow they could patch things up between them.

"Excuse me, but you're burning the bacon," Cornelius pointed out.

Aunt Phil quickly turned back to the stove and removed the frying pan from the burner.

"Okay. I'll help," Nate said at last.

Over her shoulder, Aunt Phil gave him a tired smile. For the first time, he realized she'd aged considerably over the past few hours. Her face was normally full of energy and quick to smile, but now, now there were lines around her mouth and her cheeks sagged a bit.

"Come on, then. Let's get started." She put their breakfast on plates and carried them with her as she led him into her big, cluttered library. Nate had never been in this room before. Every wall was lined with bookshelves, and every shelf was stuffed with a double row of books. More books were stacked on the floor, like leaning towers. There were two large tables and a cluster of small ones, and two desks faced each other from across the room. The walls were practically papered with maps. Hundreds more were rolled up and scattered throughout the room, tucked in corners, stacked like logs on the floor, and poking out of cubbyholes.

"Wow," Nate said. "You have enough maps here to make a hundred Books of Beasts."

"Remember, Nate, Fludds have been making maps for the last five hundred years, if not more. We'll spread out here." She plunked the original *Book of Beasts* onto one of

the tables, then quickly cleared everything else away. "While I begin searching for maps we can use, why don't you scan the bookshelves and see if you can find a book with a binding that looks as much like *The Book of Beasts* as possible."

"Are the books in any sort of order?" he asked.

"Not so that you'd notice. Besides, it doesn't matter what is actually in the books—we're just looking for the closest match, cover-wise."

A few minutes later, Nate came over to the worktable and dumped a stack of four books onto it. "These were the closest I could find," he said. "None of them is exact, but they all are close. This one is the same color, but this one has the same kind of locking clasps—see?"

"Excellent. We'll take what we need from each of them. Here. You're a better artist than I am. Can you take this map and add an extra mountain range here? Then on this map, I need you to try to cover up this pass through the mountains, then redraw an incorrect one here. Can you do that?" She scooted a box of colored pencils and a pan of paints his way.

Nate studied the maps she'd handed him. No drawing of his had ever been this important. He tried not to think

of his parents or the beasts whose lives depended on his being able to fool Obediah. "I think so," he said, then picked up a paintbrush and got to work.

And so they spent the rest of the day, furiously working at creating a perfect *imperfect* replica of *The Book of*

Beasts. Nate redrew old maps, altering landscapes, erasing valleys, and creating rivers where there were none. While he was busy with that, Aunt Phil collected pictures of the beasts for Nate to paste into the book. Using some very old parchment and altering her handwriting, she wrote up descriptions of each of the beasts. Wherever possible, she downplayed their magical properties. They stopped only once to gulp down cheese sandwiches and lukewarm tea. Aunt Phil hadn't even waited long enough for the kettle to come to a proper boil.

By the time the clock struck midnight, they had a near-perfect copy. "What do you think?" Aunt Phil asked, holding the two books side by side.

"Wow, I can't even tell which one is which," Nate said.

Cornelius waddled over and peered closely at the books. "They are remarkably similar. This plan just may work." Coming from the dodo, that was high praise indeed.

"Let's catch a few hours' shuteye," Aunt Phil said. "Tomorrow is going to be a big day and we'll need every ounce of our wits about us." She put her arm companionably around Nate's shoulders, and together they went up the stairs. The warm weight of her arm on his back made him feel better, less exposed. He wasn't alone, no matter what happened. For a brief moment, he tried to imagine Aunt Phil and his parents together in the same room. He hastily shoved the image from his mind, afraid he might jinx things.

Aunt Phil stopped in front of his bedroom door. "Try to sleep, Nate. You won't be at your best unless you do, and I'll need your help if we're to pull this off." She ruffled his hair, then quickly leaned down and kissed the top of his head before hurrying down the hallway to her own bedroom.

Chapter Thirteen

*T*HEY LEFT FOR *B*ROCELIANDE FOREST AT DAYBREAK. They still hadn't heard back from any of Aunt Phil's contacts, but they couldn't wait any longer. Knowing that Obediah was safely in France, Cornelius decided to stay home this time. Nate's eyes widened in mock surprise. "What's the matter, Corny? Aren't you up for a little adventure?"

Even Aunt Phil hid a smile. "He's got you there, Cornelius."

The dodo said nothing, but he raised his beak into the air with great dignity and waddled back into the house.

They made it to Mr. Sylvan's cottage by midmorning. He came out to meet them, wringing his hands. "I'm so glad you're here," he said.

Aunt Phil hurried forward. "Why? What's wrong?"

Mr. Sylvan swallowed nervously. "I was allowed in early this morning to give Luminessa her vitamin tonic—"

"Does Obediah know she's foaling?"

The faun shook his head. "Not yet. But that's the problem. I think the baby is coming."

"Today?" Aunt Phil asked, a note of panic in her voice.

"Today."

The faun's warning lit a fire under Aunt Phil and she galloped out of the cottage. Before Nate had a chance to follow, Mr. Sylvan shoved three lumpy yellow pieces of fruit into his hand. "Here. The quince arrived. Luminessa might need a treat once this is all over."

Not wanting to lose sight of Aunt Phil, Nate shoved the strange fruit into his coat pockets, then ran to catch up.

This was the third time he'd hiked into the unicorn's bower, but the path had never seemed so long or so full of obstacles. Each time the trail switched back on itself, Nate thought of the precious minutes they were losing.

Neither he nor Aunt Phil spoke—they were too intent on getting to Obediah as quickly as they could. Even the forest itself seemed eerily quiet, as if it, too, was worried about its unicorn.

It was because of all that quiet that Nate was able to hear the muffled footstep behind him, a faint scrape against the forest floor. When he glanced over his shoulder, there was nothing there, but the leaves of the closest tree rustled slightly. Fear rippled along his arms and he quickened his pace. Whatever was following him, Nate didn't want to face it alone.

When they crossed the small stone bridge, Nate risked another glance over his shoulder. Still nothing. Just as he started to relax, he heard a very soft whuffling sound. He jerked his head back around.

There was still nothing to see, but he heard something pawing at the ground. Zeroing in on the sound, Nate's gaze fastened on two dark blue eyes peering at him from a thick bramble. One cloven hoof stuck out at the bottom.

Another unicorn? How could that be? Aunt Phil had said there was only one per forest.

The creature snorted again. It sounded angry to Nate. Remembering how ferociously Luminessa had greeted them, he itched to go hide behind Aunt Phil.

Then he remembered the quince in his pocket. A unicorn delicacy. Maybe if he left that behind, the unicorn would be happy with the treat and leave them alone. Nate plucked one of the pieces of lumpy yellow fruit from his pocket and let it drop to the ground. He hurried to catch up to Aunt Phil.

A short while later, they reached the edges of the meadow. Obediah had set up a small tent, and the uldra sat miserably in front of a campfire, roasting sausages. They could see Obediah's feet sticking out of the tent, as if he hadn't a care in the world and was taking a nap.

When they stepped out of the trees, the uldra leaped up and murmured something. The feet disappeared, and then Obediah himself came ducking out of the tent. His eyes lit up when he saw Aunt Phil and Nate. "You've brought it?" he asked.

"We have," Aunt Phil said shortly. "But before I hand over the book, I'll need to see the boy's parents."

"I told you—they're not here, but they are close by."

"How will we find them, then?"

"As soon as you hand me the book, I will release a carrier pigeon with instructions to have the boy's parents delivered to your house in Batting-at-the-Flies." He reached out for the book.

Aunt Phil set her pack down and fished out the fake *Book of Beasts*. Looking as if she'd swallowed something unpleasant, Aunt Phil handed Obediah the book.

He took it greedily, and as he rifled through the pages, he cackled with glee.

"The messenger?" Aunt Phil reminded him.

Without pulling his eyes away from the book, Obediah waved at the uldra. The little man went into the tent, then quickly returned with a small wooden cage holding a pigeon. Nate saw there was a note attached to its ankle.

"I'm sure you'll understand that we'll want to see the note before it leaves," Aunt Phil said.

Obediah inclined his head. The uldra opened the cage, removed the note from the bird's foot, and gave it to Aunt Phil to read. She gave a brisk nod and handed it back. "Everything seems to be in order."

The uldra retied the note to the pigeon, then removed his hand from the cage, leaving the door open. The bird hesitated at first, as if not believing its good fortune, then, with a flutter of wings, took to the sky. Nate watched it soar, his hopes soaring with it.

"Well," Obediah said. "As much as I hate to say goodbye, I really must be on my way." He closed the book, slipped it inside his jacket, and patted his chest. "Can't afford to take any chances with this, now, can I? Oh, and one more thing. I've decided that I'll take that unicorn horn after all. What use will all these riches be if I don't live long enough to enjoy them?"

"But you gave your word!" Aunt Phil said.

Obediah ignored her and began walking across the meadow.

Behind Nate, a twig broke, just off to his left. An exotic, spicy smell drifted into the clearing, reminding him of cinnamon. The faint sound of snorting and pawing came through the trees. Nate froze. Had the second unicorn followed them after all? He shoved his hand into his pocket and wrapped it around a quince, ready to throw it at the unicorn if need be.

When Obediah reached the far side of the meadow, he turned and smirked triumphantly at Aunt Phil. She narrowed her eyes. "Stay here, Nate," she ordered. But before she could take a step, a sleek white and crimson shape burst out of the trees behind them. The unicorn's hooves churned up the grassy earth, sending clods flying in all directions, like small mortars. Its blood red head was lowered so that the tricolor horn pointed directly at Obediah.

The uldra gave a squeal of fear and dived for the tent. Aunt Phil gaped stupidly at the unicorn galloping across the meadow, clearly not believing her eyes. Nate jumped forward and grabbed her arm, pulling her down so that they both tumbled to the ground.

At the commotion, Obediah stopped walking and turned back around. His mouth formed a large O, and then the unicorn was upon him.

There was a sickening crunch as the horn connected with Obediah's chest. The next moment, he was flying through the air as the unicorn flung him toward the trees. A loud thud had Aunt Phil wincing as he connected with something solid.

Nate kept low in the grass and watched as the unicorn galloped around the edge of the clearing a few times, whinnying out either a warning or a victory cry. It pawed once more, then held perfectly still.

"An indicus!" Aunt Phil breathed. "They really do exist."

Silence descended on the meadow. A number of minutes passed before Aunt Phil and Nate slowly inched to a standing position. The *Unicornis indicus* watched them with his dark blue eyes but made no movement toward them. Once they were on their feet, Nate pulled a quince from his pocket and held it out. A peace offering.

The unicorn took a halting step toward him, then paused. Nate didn't move. He stared into the unicorn's eyes, willing him to see that Nate meant him no harm.

The unicorn took another step, then another, until Nate could feel the soft cinnamon-scented breath on his hand. "Should we try to exchange breath with it?" he asked Aunt Phil in a whisper.

"Absolutely. I'll go first in case he resists." Moving slowly so as not to startle the beast, Aunt Phil lowered her head and blew softly into the unicorn's nostrils. He whickered faintly and twitched its ears. "Now you try, Nate."

Keeping his eyes glued to the indicus, Nate leaned forward and blew. The unicorn's nostrils quivered and he seemed to relax. "Here." Nate held the quince out.

Moving cautiously, the unicorn took the fruit between his teeth but didn't bite down. Instead, he pranced over to the path that led to Luminessa's bower.

"I think he wants us to go to Luminessa," Aunt Phil whispered.

"But why?" Nate asked.

"I think he wants to see his foal safely born," she said, a touch of wonder in her voice.

"Oh!" Nate breathed.

Together, they followed the indicus toward the path. When they reached it, the unicorn turned and led the way to the bower.

By the time they reached the rocky cliff that hid the entrance to Luminessa's bower, the indicus had disappeared. Everything was eerily quiet, and then Nate heard something. A small, tiny voice.

"There's a nice horsy. You go ahead and lick him all you like. But you ain't never putting that tongue on me again. Ever."

They hurried forward and found Luminessa in her nest, lying on her side. A very small, very spindly baby unicorn was curled up next to her. Its head was bright crimson, and its little stub of a horn was tipped in red. Greasle lay on the ground, staring up at the sky, as if exhausted.

"Greasle?" Nate whispered.

She lifted her head from the ground. "Oh, now you gets here. When all the excitement is over."

"What excitement?" Aunt Phil asked.

"That dumb horse went and had her baby, *that's* what excitement."

"So I see," Nate said. "And you took care of it all by yourself?"

"I sure did," Greasle said with a sniff. She sat up and looked at Aunt Phil. "Now I can stay with Nate, right?"

"Yes, Greasle. You have gone far above the call of duty today. And you have done something no beastologist has ever managed to do—see a baby unicorn into this world."

Greasle folded her arms. "Hmph," she said, but Nate could tell she was quite pleased with herself.

There was a loud whinny from high above them. Nate jerked his head up and saw the *Unicornis indicus* standing on the rocky cliff overhead, outlined against the blue sky. The unicorn opened his mouth and dropped the quince so that it landed beside Luminessa. She looked up at her mate and whinnied back. He nodded his horn once, then turned and disappeared.

Nate wondered if any human would ever see him again.

Chapter Fourteen

THE SHORT PLANE RIDE BACK to Batting-at-the-Flies was the longest of Nate's life. He was so full of hope and excitement, he could barely sit still. Luckily, this time he didn't have to worry about Cornelius. *Faster,* his mind screamed at Aunt Phil. *Fly faster.* At last they left the blue gray ocean far behind, and the rolling green hills and small patches of forest near Batting-at-the-Flies came into view. Nate leaned over the side of the cockpit as far as he dared, keeping an eye out for the house. There it was! He squinted, hoping his parents would be waiting for him outside, looking up and waving at the plane.

But when they got close enough, Nate could see that the yard was empty. That didn't mean anything, he told himself. After all, his parents had no way of knowing he and Aunt Phil would be coming home right at this moment. Besides, they were probably exhausted from being held prisoner for so long.

When the plane finally landed, Nate didn't even wait for it to come to a complete stop before he scrambled out of the cockpit. It rolled along the last few yards with Nate standing on the wing, clinging to the side of the plane. Aunt Phil shouted something at him, but he couldn't make out the words over the *put-put-put* of the engine and the *whop-whop* of the propeller.

When he was sure he wouldn't end up killing himself, he jumped from the wing. He landed on soft, loamy ground with a surprisingly hard thud and clack of his teeth.

"Nate!" Aunt Phil called out. But he ignored her, pushed to his feet, and ran to the back door. He opened it so hard, it crashed into the wall behind it. "Mom! Dad!" he called out. "We're back!"

There was no answer but the hollow silence of an empty house. *Asleep.* They were probably asleep, upstairs in one of the bedrooms. "Mom! Dad!" Nate called again, heading for the stairs.

As he took them two at a time, he heard Aunt Phil behind him. "Nate! I don't think they're here—"

Nate stomped his feet harder on the stairs to drown out her words. When he reached the second-floor landing, he went to the first bedroom door and threw it open. Empty. He crossed the hall and opened the second bedroom door, his heart sinking when he saw the dusty, empty room.

They were probably in Aunt Phil's room, he realized. It was the nicest and had the biggest bed. He ran to the end of the hall and opened Aunt Phil's bedroom door. It was full of maps and equipment, packs and all sorts of things, but no parents.

Nate turned and walked to his bedroom door. Of course. They were probably waiting for him in his room. That's what he would have done. Just as he reached his bedroom door, Aunt Phil appeared on the top step. "Nate," she said, her voice thick with sorrow. He looked up at her and she shook her head.

No! They *were* home. They *had* to be. He turned back to the door and opened it.

His room was empty, just like all the others.

Numb, he took three steps into the room and stopped. Aunt Phil had been right. Obediah had planned on deceiving them all along.

He felt Aunt Phil come into the room behind him. "Nate, I'm so sorry," she said, and laid a hand on his shoulder.

He jerked away from her. "Maybe they just haven't gotten here yet."

"No, Nate." Aunt Phil's voice was full of understanding. "If they were truly only a matter of hours away, they would have been here by now. Obediah was bluffing the whole time."

Anger, hot and ugly, bubbled through him. "This is your fault," he said, turning around to face her. "If you'd done exactly what he said, Obediah would have returned them. He knew you were going to trick him."

"No, Nate. Think for a minute. How would he have known what we'd planned?"

"I don't know. Maybe someone told him. Maybe that

dumb dodo told him." Nate pointed at Cornelius, who had finally made his way up the stairs and was standing in the doorway. He expected the dodo to fight back. To scold or protest. Something. Instead, he looked at Nate with sympathy.

That was the final straw. Nate's shoulders slumped and he threw himself on the bed. His eyes stung and he buried his face in his pillow.

The bed dipped as Aunt Phil sat next to him. He felt her

hand, warm and solid, on his back. "Nate. Obediah always meant to trick us. He is not clever enough to be able to catch your parents. Or hold them prisoner for any length of time. But Nate, if they are still alive, we will find them. We are Fludds, explorers and discoverers of the first degree. If there is one thing we know how to do, it is search the globe until we find what we're looking for."

Nate rolled over on the bed so that he could see Aunt Phil's face. "Do you mean it? We can go look for them?"

"Absolutely."

"So how do we find them?"

"We begin with Miss Lumpton," Aunt Phil said. "I'm certain she knows something. Especially if she's been visiting with Obediah."

"But we don't know how to get ahold of Miss Lumpton."

"You said you'd gotten her suitcase by mistake, right? Perhaps she has an identification tag or has written her address on her luggage. People often do, in case it gets lost."

Energized, Nate leaped up off his bed and went to the closet to fetch Miss Lumpton's suitcase. He grabbed the worn, shiny handle and dragged it back to the bed. Aunt Phil helped him hoist the case up. She carefully examined the outside, then shook her head. "There's nothing out here. Let's see if there's anything inside."

She snapped open the clasps, then lifted the lid and began rifling through Miss Lumpton's things. At the sound of crinkling paper, she began to search more earnestly. When her hand reappeared, it was holding a fat stack of letters.

Chapter Fifteen

AUNT PHIL UNTIED THE STACK OF LETTERS and examined the envelopes. "Nate? Remember how I told you that Fludds always write letters?"

A tiny flame of hope flared deep inside Nate. "Ye-es."

"And we thought your parents hadn't written any, because you hadn't received any?"

"Right."

"Well, here they all are." She looked up at him, her face grim. "Miss Lumpton had been keeping them."

"What?" He reached out and took the pile from her.

There, in bold black ink, was his name. Mr. Nathaniel Fludd, Upton Downs, England. The postmark of the one on top was May 17, 1925. One month after he'd last seen them.

With trembling hands, he pulled the letter from the envelope.

Dear Nate,

We miss you terribly and can't wait until you are ready to join us! But we'll write you every month and tell you all about our adventures.

*Once you hear how much
fun we're having, we know
you'll want to join us.*

They had written him. And
they *had* wanted him to join
them. He hadn't been forgot-
ten! He quickly rifled through
the stack until he found a
letter dated near his eighth
birthday. It had already been
opened—they all had—so he
pulled the letter out. The
handwriting looked cheerful,
with big fat loops and swirls.

*Dear Nate,
We are so sorry to
hear you don't want to
join us quite yet, but
we understand. Miss
Lumpton says you are*

still a bit nervous about traveling. We wish we
could make you see how wonderful it truly is.
Perhaps we should start with a short trip, hm?
We could come home and collect you, then take a
quick trip to the Alps, just to get your feet wet.
Write us back and let us know what you think
of that idea.

Dear Nate,

Oh, how I wish you were here with us! Today
we flew over the North Pole in a dirigible! Your
father and I agree that airships are our favorite
way to travel. And we think you would like it as
well. What do you say, love? Are you ready to join
us yet?

He looked up at Aunt Phil. "They had sent for me!" he said, marveling at the wonder of it, the sheer relief. They hadn't rejected him, or thought him unworthy.

Then the force of Miss Lumpton's deception hit him. "Why?" he asked Aunt Phil. "Why would Miss Lumpton hide these from me?"

Aunt Phil's face hardened. "I don't know, Nate. But she has a lot of explaining to do. Perhaps she was afraid for you. Or perhaps she was afraid of losing her position. Whatever the reason, I intend to find out."

"How?"

"Her address is printed inside the suitcase. Here. See?"

Nate leaned over and saw the address printed in small black letters. "What if she doesn't know anything?"

"Well, if nothing else, she'll have to answer to me for having deceived you all these years. And if she can't tell us anything about your parents' whereabouts, well, we'll just have to retrace their steps."

"You mean . . . ?"

"I mean, we'll start where they were last sighted, boarding the airship headed for Spitsbergen."

Nate's chest was so full of hope, he was afraid he'd float right off the bed. His parents were still out there. Even Aunt Phil believed him now. Not only that, Nate was a Fludd. And Fludds were very, very good at searching the globe and finding things.

On Unicorns

Unicornis europus

Also known as the Western unicorn, this creature is the size of a large stag or a horse, white in color, with a tufted tail, cloven hooves, and a horn two cubits long protruding from its brow. The *Unicornis europus* also includes the German eichorn, which has a shaggier mane and coarser coat and whose horn has slightly raised ridges.

It is said that the unicorn is so ferocious it cannot be taken alive. This, however, is not true. Justina Fludd, beloved young daughter of Sir Mungo Fludd, was the first to capture a unicorn without injury. No one was more surprised than she when the wild creature walked up to her, gentle as a lamb, and laid its head in her lap. Unfortunately, many unscrupulous hunters quickly learned of this weakness, and many a poor maiden was tricked into luring unicorns to greedy hunters. Since unicorns excel at seeing the truth, this left them with an abiding hatred of men, whilst having no effect on their fondness for maidens.

It is therefore extremely important that all male beastologists be introduced to known unicorns as early in their training as possible, preferably while still children. For once a unicorn knows a person's scent, it is much less likely to kill that individual. This is not absolute, however, as poor Figgis Fludd discovered in an unfortunate incident in the Black Forest where he was attacked by an eichorn with whom he had once exchanged breath.

It is useful to note that unicorns have a weakness for quince, not unlike horses with apples.

Unicornis monocerus

(also known as the Arabian carcadan and the rhinoceros)

The *Unicornis monocerus* is the one species of unicorn that thrives today. While it is still hunted for its horn, its numbers have not been decimated in the ways of the other species. It was described by Sir Mungo Fludd thusly:

It is gray in color and shaped somewhat like a bull. Only slightly smaller than an elephant, it is a large, angry beast that loves to fight. It has a boar's tail and a black horn that is one cubit long, which sprouts from its forehead and tapers to a point. It shares some attributes with pigs, as it appears to be fond of wallowing in mud and muck.

Its voice is loud and unharmonious, an assault upon the ears.

Unicornis elasmotherium

Said to dwell in the steppes of central Asia, this beast was first reported by Sir Mungo Fludd after his initial travels through that area. It has not been spotted since, and indeed, many believe that Sir Mungo did not see this beast for himself but instead reported stories told to him by the people of the steppes. It was said to have been hunted by the locals by being driven into the forests, where they would climb the trees, wait, then rain poisoned arrows down upon it.

It is related to the monocerus as the elephant is to the woolly mammoth.

A later beastologist, Gumbert Fludd, who visited the area in 1612, reported rumors of it still in existence but was unable to confirm this with an eyewitness account.

unicornis capricornis

Unicornis capricornis

Closely related to the *Unicornis europus,* the capricornis is smaller in stature with a more goatlike appearance, including a tufted beard and smaller mane. It is also significantly less aggressive than any of the other species and easier to tame. Some capricornises have even, upon occasion, been domesticated, most notably by Ninian and Palmerius Fludd. The capricornis is of hearty appetite and has been found to eat anything. Its horn, however, does not possess the powerful properties of other unicorn horns.

Unicornis indicus

This creature is found in the wilds of Asia and India and is marked differently than the other species. While it has a white body, its head is a dark red, the color of old blood, and its eyes a dark blue. Its horn, too, is different, being only one cubit in length. The horn is white at the base and black in the middle, and the pointed tip is crimson. The indicus is said to bray like a wild ass.

The bones of this creature are also distinct, for they are the color of cinnabar.

The *Unicornis indicus* was first discovered by Mauro Fludd in 1481 during his travels through Asia and India. No one has seen it since.

Unicornis qilinus

The Chinese qilin was first seen and reported by Crespi Fludd, as were many of the Chinese beasts. It has the body of a deer, the head of a lion, and the legs of a horse, and its body is covered in green scales. A long, curved horn is what marks this as a member of the unicorn family, although there have been disputes among beastologists as to whether it is truly a unicorn or rather, as some suspect, a horned chimera.

In spite of its most fearsome appearance, the qilin is reputed to have a gentle nature. Indeed, it even goes so far as to avoid crushing so much as a blade of grass beneath its feet. Local myth maintains that the qilin was sacred to the local gods. Seeing a qilin is rumored to be a sign of great good fortune.

Unicornis kirinus

While still retaining many of the characteristics of the Chinese qilin, the Japanese kirin is somewhat more closely related to the Western unicorn. It was first identified by Flavius Fludd, then further studied by Albertus Fludd in 1563. It is not to be confused with the modern-day giraffe, which the Japanese also call *kirin*.

Japanese kirin

Unicornis narwhalus
(also known as
the monodon monocerus)

The narwhal is the unicorn of the deep, preferring the frigid oceans of the north. It weighs about half as much as a small elephant and is a mottled black and white color. When first born, its skin is darker, and it lightens with age. The narwhal's horn is five to seven cubits in length, and it is not a true horn at all, but rather a tusk or tooth. The first Fludds to have spotted the narwhal were Francis Fludd in his exploration of Greenland and Norbert Fludd during his searching for the Northwest Passage.

The narwhal is a wild creature, and to date, not a single one has been able to survive in captivity.

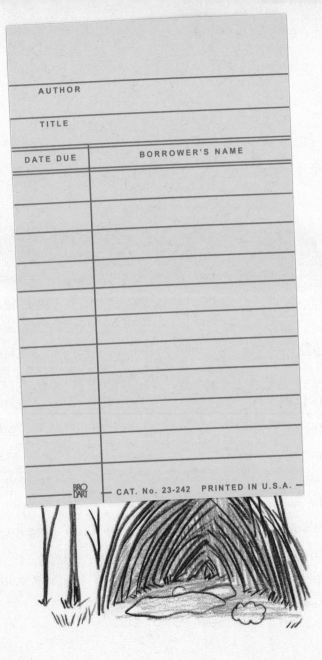

AUTHOR

TITLE

DATE DUE	BORROWER'S NAME

BRO DART — CAT. No. 23-242   PRINTED IN U.S.A. —